On the Ropes of Scandal

The Boxers of Brook Street
Book 3

Sandra Sookoo

ARE YOU SIGNED UP FOR DRAGONBLADE'S BLOG?

You'll get the latest news and information on exclusive giveaways, exclusive excerpts, coming releases, sales, free books, cover reveals and more.

Check out our complete list of authors, too!

No spam, no junk. That's a promise!

Sign Up Here

www.dragonbladepublishing.com

Dearest Reader;

Thank you for your support of a small press. At Dragonblade Publishing, we strive to bring you the highest quality Historical Romance from some of the best authors in the business. Without your support, there is no 'us', so we sincerely hope you adore these stories and find some new favorite authors along the way.

Happy Reading!

CEO, Dragonblade Publishing

Additional Dragonblade books by Author Sandra Sookoo

The Boxers of Brook Street Series
With Love in Their Corner (Book 1)
Go Down Swinging for Love (Book 2)
On the Ropes of Scandal (Book 3)

The Hasting Sisters Series
The Devil's Game (Book 1)
A Second Summertime Courtship (Book 2)
An Impossible Match (Book 3)

Willful Winterbournes Series
Romancing Miss Quill (Book 1)
Pursuing Mr. Mattingly (Book 2)
Courting Lady Yeardly (Book 3)
Guarding the Widow Pellingham (Book 4)
Bedeviling Major Kenton (Book 5)
Charming Miss Standish (Book 6)
Teasing Miss Atherby (Novella)

The Storme Brother Series
The Soul of a Storme (Book 1)
The Heart of a Storme (Book 2)
The Look of a Storme (Book 3)
The Sting of a Storme (Book 4)
The Touch of a Storme (Book 5)
The Fury of a Storme (Book 6)
Much Ado About a Storme (Novella)
A Storme's First Noelle (Novella)
A Storme's Christmas Legacy (Novella)

Chapter One

October 10, 1817
Stapleton House
Marylebone, Mayfair
London, England

G OOD GOD, *I am not in the appropriate mindset for this nonsense today.*

The last thing Duncan Stapleton—Lord Frampton if one was being strictly and socially correct—wanted right this minute was to talk with his brothers. In point of fact, he'd spent last evening gaming with some of his friends, and during those hours, he drank rather more heavily than he should have, so that had given him a headache upon waking earlier this day that insisted upon lingering now.

Even worse was having his mother as well as his brothers' wives in attendance for this family dinner—which had been enacted upon the Stapleton connection ever since Lewis, his oldest brother, had married in the summer—and quite frankly, he couldn't help but think this particular a family meeting had been called in order to force him to do *something* with his life.

And to tamp down on his penchant for scandal.

"Good evening, everyone." He threw a glance about the drawing room. Though he wasn't happy to be there, he had to admit, with the ladies present in their colorful gowns, the gathering had a more pleasant air than when it had only been his brothers.

On the other hand, since his brothers had both met and married their wives earlier in the summer, there was never a break from having *someone* underfoot. His new sisters-in-law had integrated into the day-to-day operations of the boxing salon that he and his brothers ran. Lewis' wife Cecilia was good with numbers and ledgers. More and more she was lending a hand so that his middle brother Alexander wouldn't need to continue with that task. It was a good fit, and since Lewis had injured himself that summer in the boxing ring, he no longer entered illegal bare knuckle matches for the prize purses.

Which left that responsibility to him—Duncan—and Alexander, whose skill and talent therein weren't as good.

Lewis grinned. "Lovely to have you, Duncan. Brandy?" He headed toward the sideboard as he spoke.

"Uh, I'd rather have tea, if you don't mind," he responded as he moved to the low table between the sofas where his mother and sisters-in-law sat. "I'm suffering a megrim and need something more bracing than spirits."

His mother tsked her tongue. "All of that to say you are hungover." She shook her head. "Why can you not behave for once?"

Duncan rested his gaze on his mother as he sat beside Lewis' wife. "Where is the fun in that?" Then he leaned forward and helped himself to a cup of what appeared to be tepid tea from the silver tray. It didn't matter that he hadn't put sugar or cream in the beverage; he merely needed it straight and preferably strong.

"Leave off, Mama," Alexander said, with a grin and then a wink at his wife, Lydia. "Duncan is the baby of the family. You know how young men are in the fact they can't hold their liquor and get easily distracted by shiny things like coin."

He glared at his brother. "Do shut up."

To be fair, Alexander did much for the salon and served as the manager most days. A couple times a month, he entered prize fights held in Surrey, but he wasn't as skilled a boxer as Lewis, or if Duncan were being honest, him. That just wasn't who Alexander was, and there was nothing wrong with that. Lewis taught private boxing lessons while Duncan and Alexander ran the salon, conducted lessons for men who paid for them, or they allowed clients to use the salon for their own personal training.

It wasn't a bad life, but it was… uninteresting.

"I'm teasing you, Duncan," Alexander said with a chuckle, as Lewis handed him a glass of brandy. "But you must admit, you're a horrible steward of coin, and you have no good judgment when it comes to vices."

He drained the tea from his cup. "I'm a third son. It's practically expected."

The one saving grace? As of yet, neither Lewis nor Alexander had announced that their wives were increasing, but Duncan wouldn't be surprised if the news came soon, for they were both besotted with their chosen spouses. And then what would that mean for him as well as the boxing salon? He refused to be the only one working to make it a success merely because he wasn't married. Not that he wouldn't be happy for his brothers, but such a thing would bring to light how empty and frivolous his own existence was.

As he leaned forward and refilled his teacup, he frowned. Yet the fact that he'd been summoned to Lewis' home for dinner as well as this family meeting didn't bode well.

God, please don't announce a pregnancy.

"Don't let your brothers bully you," Lydia said as she pushed a pin back into her upswept red hair. "They both forget that they were once young men who had their irresponsible moments." She grinned and shrugged. "You'll come out of it sooner or later."

Lewis cleared his throat. "We'd like that to happen sooner."

Why was his oldest brother such a prick? He eyed Lewis with a frown. Of them all, he resembled their deceased father the most. Though their father was a famous bare-knuckle boxer who made the Stapleton name familiar in those circles, they had all been taught how to box and fight. Lewis still labored beneath the responsibilities of being the earl... with nearly empty coffers, which was why they'd opened the salon to begin with.

"Thank you, Lydia. That's appreciated." He took a healthy swig of the tepid tea. "What's this about, then?" he asked as he included his brothers and mother in his glance. "Since dinner is quite pedestrian, and the whole family is here, I can't help but think I have somehow curried disfavor with all or some of you. Out with it so we can all move forward."

Before his head ached even more, possibly due to the fact that he felt largely unappreciated in the family. Even though it was through his efforts at promoting the salon that the business brought in more profits each month, and it was *his* ability to charm and secure monetary backers for the prize fights as well as investors. Neither brother had outright thanked him for that work.

They can both piss off.

Lewis drained his glass then set it on a nearby ivory-inlaid table. "Of course you aren't here for dressing downs or lectures." When their mother frowned, he quickly added, "Well, we do need to address your latest scandal."

"I'm afraid you'll need to be more specific," Duncan shot off without thinking. "I usually have more than one happening at any given time."

As Cecilia gasped, Lewis narrowed his eyes. "The opera singer," his brother said, without preamble. "Is she under your protection?"

"Uh, she is not. In fact, when I offered, she said she might be a singer, but her dignity prevented her from accepting such a position from a man with pockets nearly to let." He couldn't help his grin. "Damn, but she was a looker, though, and she had no qualms warming my bed." And he did have two glorious nights with her about a month ago. Why the rumors were only just coming to light, he couldn't say.

"For shame, Duncan," his mother said, with shock in her

voice. "That is nothing to be proud of, and women like that should be avoided at all costs."

"Then you haven't listened to some of my friends." Of course, that skirted a line, but he didn't care. "You already know what sort of man I am. Nothing has changed in that regard."

"Yes, and that is the problem," Lewis said as he rubbed a hand along the side of his face. Of all the brothers, his light brown hair was the shortest. "Now that the family is changing and since Alex and I are both married, as well as for the good of the salon, we are hoping to keep scandal away from the Stapleton name." He blew out a breath. "To be blunt, your affairs are usually scandalous, and you are more often than not with your pockets to let, so vendors come to me to pay your bills. Things need to change."

Finally, they'd reached the meat of the matter. After he'd drained his second cup of tea, he rested the cup in the sauce on the table. "If you hadn't cut off my funding, that wouldn't be an issue." Thank God he'd paid for his rooms at The Albany six months in advance or else this conversation would have a whole different outcome. And he refused—refused!—to beg an income off his brother.

Lewis glared. "You know why I had to do it. Yes, the salon has been steadily gaining support since we opened in June, but it's not yet enough to pay the debts Papa left me, and now both Alexander and I both have new responsibilities that require more coin."

And there it was. The hinting that he was a drain to the family coffers. "So I'm the rubbish one because I have maintained by bachelor status?"

Lydia chuckled. "Well, according to polite society, bachelors are leeches."

He ignored her.

"Be that as it may..." Alexander snorted. "Here's the truth that my wife was hinting at. You are a rake, man. The gossip-mongers adore you, for you never fail to, well... fail spectacularly with the ladies, leaving a trail of broken hearts behind—single and married—as well as equally irate husbands to some of them."

"Ha." Duncan shrugged and kept his emotions hidden. He leaned back on the elegant sofa, and then rested an ankle on a knee, hoping he appeared more nonchalant than he felt. "Can I help it if those men didn't know how to properly satisfy their wives? Or, additionally, that ladies find me charming? What kind of man would I be if I disappointed them?"

Lewis snorted. "A man less apt to catch the pox or some other dreaded disease that could kill you."

Both his mother as well as Cecilia gasped, while Alexander's wife, the new Lady Wexford, chuckled.

Of course, it was Lydia who answered. "The earl isn't wrong. I've studied medicine for a long time. Men, especially, are prone to contracting quite nasty things when they've visited too many beds."

Oh, God.

Heat went up the back of Duncan's neck. How did they even come to this topic? "I am careful of who I'm intimate with."

"That doesn't matter," Lewis went on with a wave of his hand. "The family grows weary of your scandals and on-dits. The best course is if you find honest work to give you a sense of purpose."

What was this, then? Hot anger rose in his chest. "I bring in quite enough money for the salon, and I've won more than enough bouts recently to keep that funding flowing." His downfall was expensive women and the lure of the gaming tables.

And too much high quality, imported brandy.

When his mother cleared her throat, all eyes went to the dowager. "Or, barring that, you can join the church."

After a few moments of shocked silence, hilarity erupted around the room.

"Duncan?" Alexander nearly fell off the sofa in his amusement. "Can you even imagine him as a vicar? A pious man? A man who is responsible for leading sinners to the light?"

His mother narrowed her eyes. "What's better than an example?"

Even Lewis' lips twitched. "I don't believe we need to go that far, and no, the church would kick him back, for he is *not* a penitent man."

The dowager huffed. "He could be if he but tried. Besides, having structure in his life would benefit him. Relying on being humble and caring about other people might have a profound effect on him."

What kind of shit is this?

The conversation was over. Duncan rose to his feet and brushed a piece of lint from his sleeve. "With all due respect, Mama, I am *not* joining the church. In fact, I'd rather not step foot in a church for *any* reason, thank you."

"Then go into banking, son. It should keep you busy."

He blew out a breath. "Alexander's the one with a head for numbers. Clearly, I can't take care of the income I do have, so that's also a no."

Lewis held up a hand. "Calm yourself, Duncan. I truly don't believe that is in your future either." He nodded. "However, you'll need to sort yourself out. An honest days' work. No more dropping into the salon when it suits you around your other... activities. You'll come in and open the salon, help Alexander with lessons, and then close it out with either him or me."

"Ah, but here's the rub." He refused to let his family bully him. "I *used* to do that, but I was annoyed when you fellows decided your wives were more important and left me with the responsibility of running the salon by myself more times than not." What had been a three-man operation was often neglected, and he was tired of it. "Quite frankly, I never signed on to take care of everything by myself, and when I'm stuck at the salon, I don't have the freedom to talk to men who might invest in our business, which is where my talents lie."

At least his brothers had the grace to look uncomfortable. It was something.

"And if I'm being fully honest, I don't want to toil for the rest of my life for something that won't fully benefit me." If it sounded harsh, he couldn't help that.

"I understand." Alexander nodded. "That is our fault, and you're right. Just because Lewis and I are married, we shouldn't shirk our duties." He offered an apologetic smile. "I'm trying to do better."

"I'll believe it when I see it," Duncan groused.

Though Lewis exchanged a glance with his wife and then nodded, he said nothing.

"Boys, that is enough." His mother guided the direction of the conversation back to the topic at hand. "Do better, Duncan. Out of all my sons, you are the one who reminds me the most of your father." When the other two boys protested—for she'd also said the same about them at one time or another—she nodded. "It's true. Your father was handsome, charming, a quick talker, could make anyone agree with him… and he also had his failings, but he was happiest when boxing."

"I can see that." Yet Duncan shook his head. "Papa also died early and left his family with nearly empty coffers. That isn't being mindful of said family or the future."

His mother frowned. "That aside, he was a family man and would have done anything for all of us."

"Except apparently make certain we were financially secure," Alexander muttered.

"Again, enough." His mother rebuked them all, and her glare was quite fierce. "I grow weary of how you cut your father's legacy and name to ribbons. Yes, we are still climbing out of a spot of bother, but your father did his best. He always wanted you boys to speak of him fondly, and yet here you are complaining. At least you still have his holdings and properties, so practice gratitude instead."

At once, all three of them apologized.

But Duncan felt the need to defend himself. "To be clear, I'm not giving up boxing nor my position at the salon, but I do want help." He caught his brothers in his gaze. "Also, romance and love is *not* an excuse to abandon what you had before. As for the scandals…" He shrugged. "I promise to keep my comings and goings more discreet. They aren't something I can give up either. Nor should I have to. We are not Puritans."

Not that he could keep a mistress—or pay high-class courtesans—on the limited funding he possessed.

"Fine." Slowly, Lewis shook his head and agreed. "That's acceptable. None of us have the right to tell you what you can or cannot do with your life. We can only advise. As long as you keep away from the gossipmongers."

"Good." Relief twisted down Duncan's spine. "Continuing in the vein of business, I have a bout in two days in Surrey. Will you both attend?"

"Uh…" Alexander shook his head as he tugged at the knot of his cravat. "I have already made plans with my wife. We are hosting our first dinner party. Her father will attend since he'll be in London for a few days from Cambridge. Frankly, we want to make the most of the time with him and come to know each other better."

"Ah." Fair enough. "Lewis? What about you?"

His older brother frowned. "I have duties to parliament. Though the session hasn't started, I'm sponsoring an idea that I hope might someday become a law, but I need to write my speech and finish a bit of research. Possibly, I'll put in several late nights in the process. At least in this, I can do some good, more than Papa did with his seat in the Lords."

Of course, it was all quite legitimate, but that further annoyed him.

Duncan shook his head then shoved a hand through his hair, which was a few inches longer than the current fashion demanded—another rule he didn't care to follow. "Of course, when it's *me* in the ring, you two can't manage to come for support. Even after I have been there for both of you in every bout *you've* entered." Again, he felt wildly underappreciated. "I'll have to bring a friend to be my knee man and perhaps snag an urchin for my water boy."

Lewis took a few steps toward him, and when he reached out, Duncan minced away to avoid being touched. "Don't come the crab with me. I can't help that I'm an earl."

"Of course you can't; it's something we've *all* known you would be eventually." He'd even bragged about it when they'd been youths. "Just remember, the title won't be there for you when you need a human connection." As annoyance continued to fill his chest, he stormed to the door. All this drove home the fact that women in a permanent capacity in a man's life were a horrid idea. "Thank goodness I have no romantic entanglements on the horizon; at least *my* life won't be ruined."

Then he strode out of the drawing room and hit the stairs nearly at a run. He didn't need any of this in his life, and if his brothers couldn't respect him, then to hell with them.

Chapter Two

October 11, 1817
Bidwell's Bakery
Cranleigh, Surrey
England

MISS PHOEBE BIDWELL happily placed an order of cinnamon scones into brown paper and tied the parcel with twine for one of the customers in the small bakery. The sugary spicy scent of them never failed to make her smile.

"Thank you for coming, Mrs. Peters. Enjoy the scones." Then she handed the box to the last customer of the morning, and with a wave, saw the woman out of the small bakery.

"It's glad I am that the customers have trickled off because we're nearly out of most of the popular pastries," her aunt Bess said, as she wiped her brow with a handkerchief.

Aunt Bess had been her anchor in what were oftentimes turbulent seas. She was as short as Phoebe was, standing only a couple of inches over five feet, but where Phoebe possessed black, curly hair, her aunt's locks were a mousy brown shade that had her forever lamenting. Of course, these days, gray threads wove their way through the hair. The other difference between them was that Aunt Bess' figure was rather on the portly side, and Phoebe was only pleasantly plump. Those curves vexed her to be sure, but there was nothing she could do about it, for she was indeed her father's daughter.

"I agree. It has been exceptionally busy this morning."

On a typical morning, Phoebe and her aunt came into the bakery around four o'clock in an effort to freshly bake the day's pastries—scones, jam tarts, seed cakes, tea cakes, a couple of different varieties of savory and fruit-filled hand pies—and a few biscuits, as well as loaves of bread. They had done the same for a few years and had the preparations down to a routine that didn't require much thought, but it *was* easier with two people.

The good thing about that was working with her aunt brought her a feeling of fulfillment, for the good woman was the only family Phoebe had left, and most of the time, once two o'clock in the afternoon arrived, the shelves were nearly empty. Which meant they could both go home and enjoy the remainder of the day.

"At least we know our baked goods are still popular." When Aunt Bess smiled, her round face relaxed. The Bidwell blue eyes they both shared twinkled. "Go ahead and close up for the day. Then come into the back room with me and we'll have tea."

Phoebe's stomach rumbled. "Good idea. I've been so busy wrapping up pastries and bread that I have had a moment to myself." As she wiped her hands on her pinafore apron, she moved over the worn hardwood floor to the door. Then she turned the key in the lock and flipped a hand-painted sign that hung in the front window so that it reflected that the bakery was closed until the next morning.

As she glanced out the window, her gaze fell onto Mr. Hannerford. He was a widower in his late thirties with two small children. His wife had died a few years before of the same fever and sickness that had taken her mother and sister as it had swept through the village. As of late, he had been trying to flirt with her, and she rather suspected he wanted her for his second wife to take care of his children.

"Ugh. Mr. Hannerford is in the square, no doubt waiting for me to lock up the bakery and walk home." A few times a week, he tried to escort her there, so a few times a week, she had to steel herself to deflect his advances.

Aunt Bess chuckled. "He is quite determined to marry you."

"He is, but not for romantic purposes, merely wishes for a mother to his children." And from all she'd observed of the pair—one boy and one girl under the ages of eight—they were quite the handful. "I am not interested in being an immediate mother after I wed someone," she said as she went behind the bakery counter and then ducked into the back room with her aunt. It served as a sitting room with a tiny kitchen on one side. Though there were rooms upstairs of a cozy apartment with a small room that served as a drawing room, as well as two small bedchambers, she and her aunt lived in a cottage a mile's walk from the bakery. It wasn't grand by any stretch of the imagination, but it was safe and had a homey feel that gave her security. "In fact, I want a romance. I want to enjoy the time with anyone I marry."

"Well, you should know about love and romance," her aunt said with another chuckle as she moved to the small stove to set the kettle on to heat. "You've been engaged twice."

"I know." Phoebe removed her apron, hung it on a wooden peg set into the wall behind the door, then she moved further into the space and collapsed into a comfortable winged-back chair upholstered with faded damask silk of blue and gold. No doubt it had been given to her by a well-to-do member of the community when they'd no longer wanted it. "It's a horrible thing to remember."

She was four and twenty, and she had already seen far too much death in that short lifetime. Three years ago, her mother and younger sister had perished from a sickness that had swept through with virulent symptoms that affected the lungs. The year before that, her second fiancé had been killed in the Napoleonic wars. His parents were from a village across Surrey, and they hadn't been forthcoming on the details, but they had told her that he'd been one of the deceased soldiers in the Peninsular War. Before *that*, her father, brother, and her first fiancé had all been killed in the war, and the same battle for that matter.

All that death since she'd been a young woman of nineteen. It wasn't right and it certainly wasn't fair, but then, that was life at times.

"I agree with you on that count, dear." Aunt Bess nodded as she puttered about, putting tea leaves into the bottom of the tea pot and then putting various dishes on a wooden tray. "I thought losing my brother in that damned war was going to be in the end of me, but then losing everyone else too? Now I'm determined to live out of spite to fate."

"There are times when I feel that way too, but most days, I feel numb, or else I just have no interest in anything at all." Except baking. There was something special regarding manipulating ingredients that made food stuffs people enjoyed.

"I wouldn't fret, dear. Sooner or later, you will find a new man, and those feelings will return, then before you know it, you'll find yourself married."

"Hmm. That is asking much out of me and my heart. I'm not certain I'm strong enough to survive a loss again." She frowned while her aunt brought over the tea service and rested it on a low table in front of both winged-back chairs. "The grief is overwhelming some days."

And if she never allowed herself close to anyone again, that was one way to combat it.

"It is one reason I've never married myself." She poured out a cup and then offered it to Phoebe. "I've always been of a mind that one person shouldn't need to bear so much grief or heartache in a lifetime." She shrugged. "Of course, that could be the wrong way to think about things, for isn't grief the price we pay for love?"

"Folks say that, but is it one of those platitudes one says in lieu of something else? Or that they don't know *what* to say?" Phoebe wrapped her hands around the porcelain cup. She was grateful for the warmth of the tea, for there was definitely a hint of autumn in the air.

"More often than not, I rather believe people don't know what to say." For a bit, the two enjoyed tea in silence, and of course the cakes on the tray had been made by her aunt. "You know, with your skill in baking, it should be a simple enough task for you nab a man if you wished."

Phoebe rolled her eyes to the ceiling before focusing again on her aunt. "Surely all men don't make decisions based on the fullness of their bellies."

"No, of course not." Her aunt shook her head. "They made them based on the *fullness* of their members. From my experience, men are guided with their pricks, and by the time they come to their senses, it's too late, and the scandal has already happened. To be honest, far too many marriages occur because of scandal over love." When Phoebe's cheeks heated, Aunt Bess laughed. "Oh, come now, my girl. After two fiancés, surely you still don't have maidenly shocks."

"Aunt Bess!" The heat intensified. "I did none of those things with either John or George." More's the pity, that, for had she known that she would still be unmatched at this age and after so much, she would have let those men do more with her than kissing. She slid a glance to the older woman. "Never tell me that you aren't a proper spinster."

"A lady never tells," her aunt said with a chuckle.

"Except, you don't carry that title, Auntie," Phoebe quickly pointed out with a laugh of her own. Though her father—Bess' brother—had been a decent man, he certainly hadn't been a lord, nor did he hold any other title. She took a sip of her tea. "I aspire to be you, I think. You've kept these secrets for so many years and didn't bat an eye about it." After another sip, she continued. "I am beginning to wonder if I will ever know about such things as what goes on between men and women."

"A whole lot of nonsense, that's what." Her aunt sipped her tea. "And some men aren't that skilled in pleasuring women, so it's a huge waste of a tup."

Dear heavens. She hadn't known that about her aunt. "How do you, uh, know when a man *is* skilled in such things?"

"Well, for one, they aren't going to look like Mr. Hannerford." She winked as she drained her teacup. "Also, men who know a thing or two will be charming. They'll be handsome—perhaps even dangerously so—and they'll know exactly how to smile at you so that you'll give them anything they want."

"Men like that sound as if they're criminals."

Aunt Bess chuckled. "Sometimes they are, but that's what also makes them attractive."

This was quite interesting information. "What else can you tell me?"

She narrowed her eyes. "Why?"

Phoebe shrugged. "In the event that I'd ever want to attract a man again. And not the type like Mr. Hannerford," she added with a little shiver. "I might want a family someday, but I want children on my own terms, not given to me immediately after a wedding ceremony."

"Oh, I don't blame you, and especially when referring to Mr. Hannerford. He's as oily as they come. Why, one look at him will tell you that he won't be faithful. It's probably an act of God that Mrs. Hannerford left this world early."

"Don't say that. She has two children." It was a sad story, of course, but she wasn't so sympathetic—or desperate for a husband—that she'd marry their father.

"God rest her soul and keep theirs, then." Aunt Bess' eyes sparkled again. "Why are you so curious suddenly? You and I seldom talk about men."

Slowly, Phoebe finished the remainder of the tea in her cup. "I still persist in dreaming of having a husband and perhaps a family. As Papa always told me, I should hope for a man of average looks and average intelligence."

"Why in the world would he say that?"

She shrugged. "Because if I tried to land a man with a title, resentment would set in for both of us and class divide would finish us off." That was the sad reality of their world. "He reminded me if the marriage failed, any children would go to the man's family, and I would have nothing."

"That sounds like my brother. Always giving harsh statements without insulation." Aunt Bess shook her head. "Well, I'm going to give you some of my advice." She drained her teacup then rested it on the saucer and put both on the table in front of her. "In matters of the heart and romance, there are no rules. You'll fall in love with the man you are fated to, despite what he is and what you are."

"What if that match is all wrong through society's eyes?"

"In the words of my dear brother, society can go hang." Her aunt nodded as if that put a period to the inquiry. "In short, don't worry about anything like that if you should wish to try and attract a new man into your life. If said man sets a spark to your soul, then by all means, pursue him if you can."

Phoebe frowned. "That doesn't make sense, for what if he's a bounder or has pockets to let? I don't wish to struggle merely to survive even if I do fall in love with said man."

"Only you can decide that, but since we are speaking of a theoretical husband, consider this. The pair of you can always find ways to make a living or bring in an income, but how often will true love come your way?" One of her aunt's eyebrows rose in question. "Would you be haunted for the remainder of your days if you turned said man away merely due to the contents of his pockets instead of his intentions?"

For long moments, Phoebe remained silent as she thought over the words. "Why is it so difficult to know what to do?"

"Because life makes it so." Aunt Bess shrugged. "It is full of decisions, which makes it our responsibility to puzzle out if we wish to be comfortable or happy, if we wish to have excitement in our existence or security."

"Why can we not have both?"

"From my experience, things don't work out that way, but you can certainly try."

Phoebe nodded. "What is the real reason you never married,

Aunt Bess?"

Her aunt dropped her gaze to the tea tray. "It's quite pedestrian, truly." Then she offered a soft smile. "Many years ago, I fell in love with a man who was completely wrong for me and the quiet life I'd made for myself here. It was only after I'd told him of my feelings that he revealed he was already engaged to a woman his family deemed more acceptable, for she had a large dowry where I did not."

"Oh, that is so sad!" Phoebe laid a hand on her aunt's. "But you just told me to go after a love that lit my soul regardless of what society wanted."

"Do as I say, not as I do?" The older woman shrugged. "Oh, I argued and pleaded with the gentleman in question, but he was adamant, even though he did admit his heart belonged to me."

A gasp came from Phoebe. "But if he was in love with you, why would he toss that away?"

"Society and responsibilities are sometimes difficult to ignore. And in the end, coin does make the world go 'round, unfortunately. We are either chasing it, going without it, or have more of it than we know what to do with." The sadness in her eyes cleared with a soft smile. "And if we're honest with ourselves, this world is expensive to live in, so one needs to have coin in order to survive."

"Is that why you opened the bakery?"

"A bit. It keeps the loneliness at bay and keeps my hands busy." The older woman paused for the space of a few heartbeats. "But it also lets me earn my own coin, and because I am not attached, I have full control over that income without having a husband to command it. And that, my girl, is the most important lesson that I want you to learn. Fight to keep what's yours, and always be mindful of that."

In an odd way, the advice made sense, but it left much lacking. "What of love, then? Is that not something we should want or even chase?"

"Of course it is. Love is the singular most perfect state anyone can find themselves in, but it doesn't always come to us, and it usually isn't perfect at all." Her smile turned rueful. "Love just… is, and if you're fortunate enough to find it, hang onto it with both hands, Phoebe."

She nodded. "I thought myself in love twice before, but you're right. It isn't perfect, and most of the time, it's quite a messy prospect." Yet she always suspected there had to be something… more to her life than working in a bakery with her aunt and the unrelenting sadness that came in fits and bursts from mourning. "Still, I would rather know just a bit of a love that went by in a heated flash if that is all fate will allow than never knowing any sort of love fully."

"Understandable." For long moments, silence reigned between them. Eventually, Aunt Bess refreshed her teacup as well as Phoebe's. "However, don't become so desperate that you cozy up to the first man who shows an interest."

Phoebe snorted with amusement. "Then not Mr. Hannerford?" Then she dissolved into peals of laughter that her aunt joined in.

"Exactly." Her aunt nodded.

"Let's just say, I am tired of being disappointed with what life has given me, Auntie. Surely, something will need to change."

"I agree. Take heart. You are young yet, dear, and there is much life still to live. A husband will find you, I can feel it." She took a deep drag of her tea. "In the meanwhile, rumor has it that there is one of those illegal bare knuckle boxing bouts slated for tomorrow evening in a meadow not far from here. Perhaps we can box up day old pastries and sell them at a discount to some of the attendees. Clear our stock so we can start fresh the next day."

There was no doubt her aunt would forever prove a businesswoman, but Phoebe nodded. "I'll take care of it if you convince young Thomas to hawk them through the crowds. I don't fancy putting myself in position for pinches and gropes." Which had happened before when such a bout was nearby.

"I don't blame you, but I'll talk to him this afternoon when he comes with the flour delivery."

"Good." With a sigh, Phoebe finished her tea. "After this, I need to stop by the milliner's shop. The repair to my good bonnet is supposed to be finished today." As dull as her life currently was, it *was* her life, and she'd best square with it.

Chapter Three

October 12, 1817
Cranleigh, Surrey

D UNCAN FROWNED AS he surveyed the large clearing of grass where the bout would take place. How long would it be for this sport to cease being illegal and for boxers to compete in a ready-made ring instead of a wildflower meadow that, more often than not, held a handful of cows? Since bare-knuckle boxing, especially for profit, was illegal within the bounds of London proper, most bouts took place outside the limits in the country. The sites were often farm fields, or clearings—even better—for sometimes thousands of spectators would assemble.

Were there thousands this evening? He glanced at the growing crowd of spectators as it swelled. Not necessarily, but there were certainly hundreds. Of course his name didn't bring in the numbers like Lewis did, but he was still a Stapleton, damn it. Didn't that mean something? Shaking his head, he watched as the assembling crowds formed a circle around the roped off section of the meadows that would serve as the boxing ring. And though he'd done this countless times, his nerves crawled beneath his skin.

The question was why. It wasn't as if this was his first time fighting. Perhaps it was because he was without the support of his brothers. The damned bounders. Every time they came out to fight, Duncan had been there to take wagers and hype the crowd in a Stapleton's favor, but when it came to him being in the ring? Where were they? Weak, from being domesticated, that's where, had no thoughts of their own, and their spines must have dissolved as soon as those vows had been spoken.

Damned women who changed them.

Well, they could both piss off. When he won the prize purse today, he'd keep the proceeds to fund his own damned life. Still, he blew out a breath as he shoved the fingers of one hand through his longish hair.

Excitement buzzed through his insides to mix with the anxiety. Since it had only taken a couple of hours to travel from London to the area where the bout was being held, he'd felt no travel fatigue, which was good. A tired fighter was a doomed fighter. When a youth sauntered over to him, he tamped down on the urge to show his annoyance. It wasn't the boy's fault Duncan's brothers were arseholes.

"Young Thomas, I presume?" he asked as he raked his gaze up and down the young man's form. He'd sent his driver back to London with the caveat that he intended to stay in an inn within the area, for he fully expected to win, and that meant he would curry favor with the village beauties. Having a willing bedmate would be just the thing to help him celebrate, then he would return to London and brag to his brothers.

"Aye. One of the judges for this event told me you were in need of a knee man or at the least a water boy. Will I do?" Probably not more than fifteen, the boy was tall and gangly, as if he didn't know what to do with his long limbs quite yet. His mop of sandy-blond hair had a mind of its own, and in the soft breeze, the short locks went every which way, but his mossy eyes were bright and his grin ready.

"You absolutely will." Hell, he'd served the same purpose for Lewis when his older brother had first started his bare-knuckle boxing career. "How much do you know about boxing bouts?"

"I know enough." He drummed his fingers against his thigh.

"Attend 'em when I can if they come to Cranleigh. Saw the earl fight a couple of years ago here in this field."

"Ah." That must have been Lewis, since their father had been dead nigh onto three years. "You'll do."

"Good enough." The boy nodded. "As long as you let me sell some of Miss Bidwell's pastries in the lulls. She asked me to help her bakery this evening too. And I welcome the bit of coin just now. Going up to London tomorrow to visit my brother for a week. He's taking me to a counting house to see if I'll be fit to work there next spring."

"Interesting." At this point, Duncan didn't care what the young man's aspirations in life were. Clearly, he, himself, wasn't important enough to have anyone's full attention… even that of a knee man or essentially a water boy. "Do whatever you need." If luck were with him, perhaps he could put down his opponent quickly.

The young man nodded. "If you don't mind me saying, Mr. Stapleton—"

"Lord Frampton," Duncan felt the need to correct him. It meant nothing, of course, but that was who he was.

"Er, right." Young Thomas nodded. "Lord Frampton. If you don't mind me saying, you seem green about the gills. I thought you Stapletons were used to bouts."

"We are, of course, but there's something about this one that has my guts in knots." As he spoke, he watched a couple of men—sponsors of the event if their expertly tailored suits were any indication—walk the meadow between the ropes. One of the men checked the sturdiness of the posts that had been driven into the ground that secured the ropes of the ring. "Not as large as the crowd if Lewis—the earl—was fighting." His confidence wavered. "I'd rather be working the crowd." Why he felt the need to admit that to a stranger, he'd never know.

"That don't matter, none," Young Thomas said. "A few hundred people here on a Sunday evening, when men should be home getting ready for roast dinners." He shrugged. "Should be a decent fight though."

"I'm sure you're right. A fight's a fight." Of course, he hoped he won the prize purse. "Do you know who my opponent is?" That was usually his job to discover for his brothers.

Young Thomas shrugged. "No one's said."

"Well, now's a good time to find out while plying the crowd with your pastries."

"Understood, Lord Frampton. Be back in a few shakes."

Shakes of what, Duncan couldn't say, and didn't care to know. While the young man loped off, he heaved a sigh, rested a hand on a post in the ground, and closed his eyes. He concentrated on regulating his breathing, for the annoyance at not having his brothers there in support made his chest tight and hot. They had always been a team. And now he'd been thrown to the wolves to preferably fend for himself in the ring?

Well, they could bloody well buggar off. I don't need them.

"Lord Frampton?"

He startled at the sound of Young Thomas' voice and popped his eyes open. "Is it time already?" Once more, his nerves crawled.

"Not yet, but I found out who your opponent is. A Mr. Sanders from London. A Black man who works as a blacksmith, and is quite muscular."

"I see." It seemed luck wouldn't shine on him this afternoon. He ducked beneath the ropes and went into the ring. "Come on, Young Thomas. The match will begin in half an hour. I need to do some warmup stretches and wrap my hands."

"Right." Poor Young Thomas nodded, though it was obvious he had no idea what Duncan meant.

As they went beneath the ropes and headed to the corner that had been assigned to him, the energy from the gathered crowd buzzed in Duncan's ears and filled his chest with confidence. He knew his skill level, and he knew what he was capable of. It didn't matter what his opponent looked like, he was a Stapleton, damn it, and he'd make a good showing.

"I might not be a boxer, my lord, but if I were you, I'd concentrate on the upcoming fight. The other man's a beat," Young Thomas warned. The sound of his voice brought Duncan out of his thoughts. "One slap of that hand will see you dead."

"I hardly think so, but don't fret. I'm preparing for the bout in my head." A hint of censure rang in his tone.

"No offense meant." The youth frowned as he poked about a wooden water bucket with a ladle inside. "It's just that you're too fancy looking to take a beating out there."

"I might not be hulking, but I'm no slouch at boxing." Truth be told, Duncan would need to use every scrap of his strength to get through to the end as he sent a curious glance to the other side of the roped off section where his opponent readied himself.

"Mr. Sanders has been in fisticuffs for a few years," the young man continued, apparently oblivious to Duncan's mood.

"And I've been in it my whole life. My experience versus his form will make it a fair fight." Duncan shook his head to clear his thoughts. "Help me get ready for the bout." He stripped to the waist and handed his clothes to Young Thomas. Then he toed off his boots and tugged off his socks, throwing the items into the corner assigned to him. The coolness of the grass beneath the soles of his feet made him feel more connected to the moment… as well as the memories of the past when he'd learned how to fight from his father. "By the by, your responsibility as my knee man is to look after my mindset, wellbeing, and water intake, and you'll also offer me a knee like a footstool so I can rest between rounds." As he spoke, he performed a series of quick stretches to warm up his upper body muscles.

"Whatever you need, Lord Frampton," the young man said with a nod.

"Good." Duncan wound strips of linen about his hands, which would help to cushion the blows, and if he was fortunate, prevent broken or badly busted knuckles. When he was finished, Young Thomas tied off the ends. "I'm ready."

"All to the good, my lord." He glanced at the opposite side of the makeshift ring where Duncan's opponent was getting ready as well. "Sanders is a large man, yes, but you look like you'll have more upper body strength, and you're smaller, so you'll be quicker."

Duncan nodded. "Decent observation. Nicely done, Thomas."

The young man grinned. "Thank you."

A shrill whistle blast pierced the air and scattered Duncan's thoughts.

He blew out a breath. "Wish me luck."

A tall man stood in the middle of the boxing square and held up a hand. "We're about to begin." When the noise from the crowd died down somewhat, he continued, "Today's match is between a favorite boxer from London, Lord Frampton, but you know him as Duncan Stapleton, youngest son of the famous boxer, George Stapleton." A roar erupted from the spectators. "And his opponent for this bout, the man who makes some of the most impressive axes and fireplace tools on his anvil, Mr. Darius Sanders. He's relatively new to the bare-knuckle circuit, but he's quite the contender." Another cheer, less intense than before, rose from the crowd.

Clearly, some of them recognized the other man's name.

As the tall man gave a bit of a speech to thank sponsors as well as the boxers, Duncan moved his gaze over the crowd. "Best get to it, hmm?" After exchanging a glance with his makeshift knee man, Duncan moved toward the judge in the center of the roped off ring.

Sanders came toward the judge from his side of the ring—a tall man with curly black hair that sat close against his head, and a sprinkling of hair on his chest that did nothing to hide how well defined his form was. Or how powerful his strikes would be.

"I wonder if you'll last even two rounds, Lord Frampton," Sanders said, with a fair amount of cockiness. "You're on the puny side, aren't you?"

What a prick. "I do well enough, and you know what they

say about the intelligence of big men." Duncan flexed his hands, then lifted his arms above his head and stretched again. "And how good can you be if I've never heard of you?"

The other man sneered. "That might be true, but after today, you *will* remember my name."

"We shall see." Confidence flowed through Duncan's veins. Seconds later, he assumed his first position, fists at the ready, body taut and balanced, feet a shoulder's width apart, just as his father had taught him. "I'll try not to wreck your face and form too badly. Still need to wield that hammer, eh?"

A whistle blast split the air. The squat and round judge shouted, "Rounds will continue until one man is put on the ground and unable to stand after three seconds. Go!"

Duncan and his opponent circled each other, prowled through the meadow grass and flowers of the eight-foot by eight-foot, roped-off area. The judge waited in one of the unoccupied corners. How best to bring Sanders down? Anticipation rode his spine while worry pulled knots in his stomach. He threw the first punch. It connected solidly with the other man's cheek and threw his head back, but not that much.

"You will need to do better than that." Sanders grinned as he struck out with a fist. "Naught but an annoying insect."

"Until I sting." Duncan minced away, much to the crowd's roar of approval. "I've much more to show you." He swung a fist, but the other man dodged the punch while continuing to circle him.

"I thought you Stapleton brothers were more formidable." Sanders darted with a fast uppercut to Duncan's chin that jarred his teeth together. "You must be the runt." Another quick right hook to the jaw had his vision wavering.

"Prick." Pain exploded through his face and the metallic taste of blood flooded his mouth, but he held his ground and returned punches. "You have no idea what I'm capable of."

Then they were into the meat of the first round as blows rained and fists pummeled, landing on solid flesh in rhythmic intervals. One of his jabs sent Sanders staggering backward, but the man recovered and came at him with fists flying and unfortunately finding purchase in various places on Duncan's body. He didn't give quarter, and his defense wasn't one to sneeze at.

As the sound of fists thudding into bodies echoed in his ears, he marked the time with fast footwork and more than a few curses. His opponent, though muscled, slightly favored his left side, and there was a bit of a burn mark on the ribs there. Interesting.

Finally, the round was called, which was just in time, since his chest hurt and his lungs slightly burned.

Grateful for the brief reprieve, Duncan retreated to his corner, as did his opponent. "Sanders is damned good and has one hell of a right hook." He perched upon Young Thomas' knee as various portions of his body throbbed in pain. "However, he's not a Stapleton."

"Just stay a step ahead." The youth handed him a ladle of cool water from an oaken bucket. "Sanders is slow with his feet once he's winded."

Surprise went through Duncan's chest. "Good observation." He wiped sweat from his brow with the back of his hand. After taking a deep sip from the ladle, he gave it back to the youth. "He's also favoring his left side."

"Then that's when you punch." Young Thomas rubbed the muscles in Duncan's shoulders. "At least, that's what I assume."

He snorted. "You're not wrong."

Another whistle blast announced the start of round two.

"Shit." With a groan, Duncan stood. He returned to the middle of the ring to face off with his opponent once more.

"You are a mere ant, Frampton." A cut on his left pectoral glittered with blood. His fingers glanced over the burn wound on his ribcage. "I need that prize purse."

"So do I," he tossed back, and because he might be a wee bit desperate for that coin, he lit out with a jab to the man's left ribcage.

Though Sanders retreated a few steps, he recovered nicely with a hard uppercut to Duncan's jaw that had him staggering backward. The crowd roared, and as one entity they surged forward. Wavering support was damned annoying, yet, people loved blood, and they enjoyed making coin on a wager to see more of it. Pain exploded through his head, but he kept his feet. Reminding himself this wasn't a drawing room and there was no need for charming grins or empty platitudes, Duncan darted toward his opponent with a growl. He landed two quick jabs to Sanders' cheeks and left ribcage, where his fist hit the burn mark.

The blacksmith gasped and winced. He retreated before gathering himself and charging at Duncan to once more exchange blows. "You're a fool, Frampton."

"That's the most complimentary thing I've been called recently." Again and again, Duncan drilled his fists into the other man's body, making certain to land them into the left side of his ribcage and face, but the boxer wouldn't fall, even after pain lined his face. Blood lay smeared over his chest.

Sanders got off a few good punches of his own, but Duncan kept his feet through sheer stubborn determination, regardless of the damn pain cycling through his body.

"I'm the better fighter." It was something he would always believe. Then he delivered a swift right hook to the taller man's cheek that had him spinning about. "Go down, damn it."

"Not tonight, you damned nob." The man wiped at his brow with a hand that had bloodied knuckles, the same as Duncan's despite the wrapping.

Before he could respond, the round was once again called without a clear victor. As he looked out over the crowds, his gaze landed on a young woman standing at the edge of the gathering. She wore a black cloak with the hood up and the folds of the garment wrapped around her, but she watched the proceedings with bright eyes. When their gazes connected, a queer sort of tingle twisted down his spine. As she gave him a nod of encouragement, he frowned before stumbling back to his corner. Then he dropped onto Young Thomas' bent knee, panting. "The blacksmith is trying my patience," he admitted in a whisper.

"But he's tiring and winded." The youth plied him with water, and Duncan gratefully drank from the ladle. "Just hold on."

"I'll try." And damn, he didn't want to think about the bout right now. In fact, all that went through his mind in this current moment was a pair of cornflower blue eyes framed by black lashes with black curly hair beneath the cloak's hood. "You from this area?" he asked, as he poured a ladle of water over his chest.

"Yes." Young Thomas nodded. "My father's a bricklayer; my mother's a seamstress."

"Ah." Duncan stood, glancing once more that the woman. When their gazes connected, she again offered a faint smile before she looked away, but heated sensation went through him from the brief exchange. "Who's that woman on the far side of the crowd?"

The youth glanced over. "Oh, that's Miss Bidwell."

Duncan frowned. "The woman you work for at the bakery?"

"No, she's the niece of that woman. One of the village's spinsters. Lost both her fiancés in the war, so the gossips say."

"Damn. Pretty thing." *What the hell is wrong with me?* He didn't need a distraction from some country bumpkin's set of intriguing eyes.

"Yes, but keeps men away, so you need to concentrate," Young Thomas whispered, and gave his shoulder a push, which refocused his wandering thoughts.

"Right. Thank you."

The judge blew his whistle again. The next round was imminent.

Duncan heaved off the young man's knee. He checked his wrapped hands as he strode to the center of the roped-off area.

"I've grown tired of this, Frampton!" Sanders came out in full-blown anger. When he engaged him into a mix of blows, jabs, and punches that left him reeling and breathless, Duncan defended as best he could.

"As have I."

When one of the blacksmith's fists drilled into Duncan's abdomen, pain swamped him, but another blow caught him in the jaw, causing him to bite the inside of his cheek. The metallic taste of blood filled his mouth again. With a hideous grin, Sanders then cuffed him on the side of the head.

"Shit." With a few blinks, Duncan roared back into motion using a quick double uppercut. Each fist found purchase in Sander's chin and left ribcage, where he ground his knuckles into the burn wound. When his opponent howled in pain, he landed a punch to the man's temple.

He didn't fall, but he jammed a fist into Duncan's midsection. "Give up, Frampton. This is embarrassing. For you."

Duncan wheezed as he stumbled backward, sucking in breaths. "Why won't you go down?"

"Because I'm the superior fighter this night." And he swung out with a powerful fist.

At the last second, Duncan ducked. Though his strength was flagging, he employed the footwork his father was famous for, to the roar of the crowd. A few moments were spent evading the other boxer and dodging blows, but he continued to bedevil the blacksmith with jabs and punches. Every movement he made brought copious amounts of pain throughout his body.

"You're done, Frampton." The other man flew at him with fast fists and rippling muscles.

Duncan defended himself as he'd been taught, but it was as if he were fighting in a snowstorm and being hit from all sides by giant shards of ice. Though he rallied a few times, punch after punch was exchanged, and Sanders didn't let up or give in.

Blood dripped down his chin from a busted lower lip. Every muscle in his body screamed out exhaustion and warning. He couldn't remember how many wounds he'd sustained, but he did some damage to his opponent. Sweat streaked into his eyes, stinging, and blurring his vision. It wet his hair, leaving it in straggly ropes, and still he fought on.

With a sound that resembled a cry of war, Sanders delivered a powerful blow to the right side of Duncan's head. One of the knuckles dug into the temple, and sent darkness flirting with the edges of his vision. "Say goodnight, Frampton." His opponent slammed a fist again into his head in the same spot, and when Duncan fell to the ground, the crowd roared. "Go back to your salon. You can use another course of training," the man said, as he peered down at him.

Pain became Duncan's new world. He lay on his back while gasping for air and hurting from countless punches. Though Young Thomas yelled at him to get to his feet, he just didn't have the strength, nor could his brain tell his limbs to cooperate. He collapsed into the sweet meadow grass and closed his eyes, then unceremoniously retched all over the ground and himself from the pain.

Eventually, the judge came near with another man Duncan assumed was a surgeon invited to the event, and he counted down from ten. He didn't move, couldn't bring himself to care, for he was rapidly losing his grip on consciousness.

"Mr. Sanders is the winner of today's bout!"

The crowd roared; it had probably been quite an entertaining evening. Blinking, he saw that the blacksmith had walked to the center of the ring with the judge, who held up one of his arms as the victor. The crowd formed tight circles around the other man as Duncan's vision wavered and darkened at the edges. As the autumn night fell around him, he was left lying in the shadows on the cool grass.

Is this where I'll die then?

"Lord Frampton." A gentle tapping on his cheeks brought him around. When he opened his eyes, it was to see Young Thomas kneeling by his side. "You must get up, my lord."

"I don't think I can." He simply hurt too much. Where were his brothers, to haul him back to a carriage and give him a bit of dignity back?

"If you don't, you're sure enough a dead man." Then he

offered him a ladle of water from the wooden bucket. "Here. Drink."

Though his throat was parched and his voice sounded raspy, he scoffed. "I'd rather have brandy," he said, as he accepted the ladle from him. After he'd drunk his fill, Duncan sat up, but the world spun around him, and the urge to retch grew strong. With a groan, he collapsed back onto the grass.

Young Thomas pointed to a clump of clothing he'd dropped on the meadow grass beside Duncan. "You should dress. It's not wholesome for you to lay here half-naked."

"In a moment." The darkness crept into his vision, and it was just confined to the edges any longer.

The youth nodded. "I'm going to hawk Miss Bidwell's pastries now, but I'll come back soon enough."

Duncan lifted a hand and waved him off. Ignoring the noise from the crowd and the men milling about, he eventually shoved to his feet and somehow managed to dress himself... but only just. He didn't care about that either. If he could manage to remain upright long enough to walk into the village and reach the room he'd rented, that would prove enough of a win for him tonight.

Except the pain wouldn't leave him, and the damned darkness was encroaching far too quickly. Perhaps having a brandy would fortify him enough to see him to his destination. Then he could return home tomorrow without a win, without a prize purse, without a woman warming his bed, and certainly without bragging rights.

Buggar everyone.

Chapter Four

Later that night

B ECAUSE PHOEBE HAD come out to watch some of the bare-knuckle boxing match, she was behind in her prepping duties for the next morning. Of course, the bakery had closed much earlier in the day, which had allowed her and Aunt Bess to spend the afternoon at their cottage.

Then, her aunt went over to share tea with a friend—as she usually did every day—and that's when Phoebe had thrown on a cloak and wandered over to the boxing match to observe for a few moments. Yes, it had been scandalous, and even more so when she unashamedly gawked at the half-naked men in the roped off section of the meadow that was the ring. Yet she hadn't looked away, and her focus had landed on Lord Frampton. Was he easy on the eyes? Of course, and never had she wanted to lick a man's chest before. It had been an overwhelming thought when she'd seen him; his flowing light brown hair that captured her attention. It practically shouted that he was a rogue, and that somehow amused her.

Just before the end of the bout, Phoebe had returned to the bakery to mix bread dough and get it on to rise for the morning. There was also the kitchen and bakery cases to clean to her aunt's specifications, because that lady would ask if the tasks had been done, even though this was their usual daily routine.

It took about two hours, but finally, with a yawn, Phoebe blew out the candles, exited the bakery, and locked the door with her worn iron key. Helping with the baking was sometimes tiring work, and all she wanted to do once she returned to the cottage she shared with her aunt was put her feet up with a hot cuppa and perhaps a book. However, she'd barely made it two storefronts down from the bakery toward the road that would lead to the path to the tiny cottage, when a man stumbled toward her.

Oh, dear.

"Go home and sleep it off," she told the man. "I, uh, have a stick and I'm not afraid to use it on you." Fearing the man was a drunk, Phoebe backtracked and then pressed herself into the bakery's doorway.

But the man kept coming. Before she had time to cast about and find something to use as a weapon, he collapsed to the ground. He lay sprawled at her feet with a gash on his forehead, bruises forming on his face, and blood at his temple. With an outstretched hand, he attempted to touch her as she shrank backward. "Do you know who I am? Or where I am?" In addition to his other wounds, he suffered busted knuckles too. "Or what the hell happened to me to make me feel like yesterday's rubbish?"

With a frown, she peered through the gathering darkness of the autumn night, and then gasped. *I recognize him!* In fact, he was one of the boxers included in the bout earlier. Of course, he had far more clothes on himself than he did when she'd last seen him. But the buttons were mismatched, and the cravat was more twisted than tied. Did he truly rely on a valet, or did he not have the mental faculties to do such small tasks?

"Uh..." Her mind spun as she scrambled to come up with a plausible story. "I'm sorry, but you don't know who you are?" How did injuries to one's head work? Did they render a man dumb to everything he'd known before?

"Clearly, I don't, and I can hardly stand upright without the world tilting," he said with a fair amount of annoyance in his voice that smacked of the aristocracy. "And it seems I already vomited on myself once. I'd rather not do it again."

"Understandable." Surreptitiously, she sniffed as she kneeled by him. He didn't smell like alcohol, which meant he hadn't visited any of the taverns in the village, but he did reek from casting up his accounts. "Ew, you need a bath."

"No doubt."

Was the urge to retch due to the pain he must be under, or the head wound itself? "And you have no idea what brought you to Cranleigh, in Surrey?"

"No." When he shook his head, he groaned and then pressed a hand to the wound at the side of his head, and he swallowed hard. "Why the devil does my head hurt and my body ache? Was I attacked?"

"More or less." It seemed he was suffering from amnesia, probably due to one or more of the blows he'd taken during the match. Would it last? Was it temporary? There was no way to know. How much to tell him? "As the winter approaches, indigents become more and more desperate."

"Did one of them attack me?"

"I wouldn't know, since I've been here most of the day."

Then she dared to touch his arm, felt for more serious injuries. Oh, dear heavens, he smelled delicious too. A hint of sandalwood with a trace of citrus, leather, and sweaty man. When one overlooked the aroma of vomit, that was. Her second fiancé used to work with horses, which had made him a valuable addition to the cavalry. Some of that scent she remembered when he used to embrace her.

I miss that so much. Not only the physical touch but the companionship, the ability to talk with someone who cared.

He watched her with glittering eyes in the darkness. "What are you not telling me?"

Knots of worry pulled in her belly. "I don't know anything about you." Beyond the fact that he was a prize fighter, and from the way he looked, he might have lost the match. That was the truth.

"That I believe." His eyes narrowed as he peered at her. "Can you help me?"

"Why should I? You're more than a bit grouchy; you look as if you've been through a war, and you don't have any coin on you." That tiny bit of exploration to his chest had confirmed there was nothing in his pockets. Despite that, need fluttered through her belly with a longing for something she barely understood but thought long dead. What would it feel like if he were to kiss her, lay her out on a bed with his body pressed atop hers?

Pull yourself together, Phoebe.

When he frowned, she almost lost control over herself, for she wanted to press her lips to his or run her fingers through his glorious hair. "Your eyes are familiar, almost haunting. So deeply blue, like lake water. Cool, inviting…" He lifted a hand and let his fingers drift over her cheek, leaving tingles behind, along with the lingering scent of blood. "I remember those eyes, but I don't remember why or how. I only know I want to."

The memory of their gazes meeting in the middle of his bout danced into her mind. Though she rather doubted that he was a man given to flowery poetry, she was a bit flattered that her eyes had made such an impression on him. Neither of her fiancés had even mentioned her eyes.

Then, a mad idea occurred to her. It would cause huge waves of scandal if she were found out, but the situation presented seemed so perfect, almost as if fate had handed her this man, with no strings attached. And this was Cranleigh, not London, so how bad could it be? Would anyone truly care?

"Oh, I…" Not able to finish the thought, Phoebe continued to stare at him as her thoughts galloped. "That was sweet of you to say."

The man on the ground shrugged. "It's true."

"A real charmer, aren't you?" She had followed society's rules for years, had done everything right, yet she'd lost two fiancés as well as her parents and her only sibling in the span of five years. She was alone except for her aunt, but that erstwhile lady had her own life and interests beyond the bakery, and she was aging.

Why shouldn't I do this?

A slow smile curved her lips, and her fingertips rested upon the fallen man's chest. Why shouldn't she put forth a couple of tiny white lies in order to carve out a piece of happiness for herself where fate had failed? He didn't remember who he was, and all it would take to keep him with her was a simple story. The villagers and her aunt would be surprised, of course, and that would take another tiny, little lie, but once the shock of it wore off, she could settle into life with this handsome and well-muscled man at her side. One who waxed poetic over her eyes.

To be fair, putting forth this bit of fiction would go beyond tiny lies, but if she kept control over them and kept them small, what harm would it do?

The more she thought about it, the more her heartbeat accelerated. Did she dare? It might be the only time in her life that she would know what it felt like to have a husband, to discover what occurred within the marriage bed, to be needed for herself. To carve out happiness after years of doing nothing but grieving for the people who'd left.

This is my chance!

Phoebe tossed caution to the proverbial winds, "Of course my eyes are familiar, you dear man," she crooned to him, as she peered down into his face. "I have been worried sick all afternoon wondering what happened to you, and from the looks of it, I'll wager you were hit in the head with a few bricks." All she needed to do was spin a convincing tale that he would believe, and then when they repeated it to her aunt or whoever else wanted to hear it, the story would be far more convincing with that repetition.

"Bricks?" Even his frown was attractive. "What does that mean?"

Damn him. Had the beatings he'd taken made him that curious, or was he truly like that in the life he'd stepped away from? Perhaps she would never know.

"Yes. Don't you remember that you laid bricks for a living?

And you're quite talented at it." She gave a nod for emphasis. "You were working on a project this week of making a kiln for the potter who lives at the opposite end of the village."

God would surely strike her dead for what she was doing, but she didn't care. She had the life she'd always wanted within her grasp, and a few more delicate strands of conversation would finish the web. Didn't she deserve that after everything? After all the sadness and disappointment?

"Well, that would explain why my hands look like a dog's breakfast." Lord Frampton held them up and stared at them as if seeing them for the first time. "Why wasn't I wearing gloves for such heavy work?"

Why was he so inquisitive? "Perhaps your hands were hot, or perhaps you had paused for a break, and an accident occurred. I wasn't there, but one of your friends came by and told me you'd wandered off. Thank goodness you instinctually knew to come here."

Oh, please just believe me and stop asking questions!

"Mmm." Slowly, the man nodded. "That makes sense."

She nearly wilted with relief.

"But *why* are you so concerned about me?" Once more his gaze fell to her face, and even in the dark, she could spy shadows in those rich brown eyes.

"Because..." Here was the test of her mettle... and her skills in lying. Phoebe ignored the sweat sliding down her spine as she cleared her throat. "Because you are my husband, William." It was a good, solid, popular name, and now that the words were out of her mouth, there was no going back. "That's why I was worried."

"Ah." He waved a hand presumably to encompass the village's shops. "Why are we here?"

Was he daft, or did his brain truly not work correctly any longer? She dug deep for patience. "I work in the bakery with my aunt. Which is located here. As I said." Phoebe gestured to the door. "You know that. We've been married for six months."

Deeper and deeper she went down the rabbit hole of dissembling. "I make the bread dough and put it on to rise overnight, and then you and I share dinner together. Most times, by the time you come down the lane into the village, I'm finished here, for you like to scrounge leftover pastries that didn't sell."

"But I couldn't, since your aunt gave them to Young Thomas to hawk at the bout."

Oh, dear heavens. Is he remembering?

As fear played icy fingers down her spine, Phoebe nodded. "True, but then, you always half-heartedly argue with her about that. You tell her the pastries should go to you for having to put up with having me as a wife." It sounded legitimate, didn't it?

"I suppose, even if this is the first I'm hearing of it." He frowned at her from his position on the ground. "But I don't recognize this place." Did that mean his memories would come and go as he healed, and the swelling went down?

It would seem she was on borrowed time. "Well, you *have* suffered a good knock to your head." As she spoke, she drifted her fingertips along his right temple, and when he winced, she tsked her tongue. "This needs to be cleaned. All your wounds do and set with a healing salve." That was the truth, at least.

"I do feel rough, but where do we live? This is a bakery."

The dear man was proving to be a trial. "I know, and I just told you that. My aunt owns this establishment. I work here, but you are a bricklayer and are always gone so early in the morning that you don't come 'round until the evening, remember?" It was insanity how well the lies flew out of her mouth. She should be horrified, but she wasn't. In fact, she looked forward to the companionship for once, to have someone—anyone—to talk to and cook for and fuss over, perhaps even love. "We live in the rooms upstairs until we have enough coin to rent a cottage." How convenient for her that there *was* a small apartment above the bakery.

To hide him. *Oh, dear Aunt Bess, please understand!*

"Come." With some effort, she helped him to stand. "You

must be hurting and exhausted. You'll be right as rain in a few days."

Slowly, he nodded. "Perhaps I do need to rest for a bit."

At least some of the difficult parts were over, but Phoebe's hand shook as she unlocked the door. "Just through the bakery proper. The stairs are in the back."

Again, he frowned, and he resembled a ghoul in the darkness. "Why were you outside with the door locked if we live here?"

Clearly, the man wasn't a nodcock, even if he suffered from amnesia. "I was going to visit Aunt Bess, to consult with her on whether I should look for you." That made sense, didn't it?

"It's a good thing you didn't already leave by the time I showed up, then."

"Yes, quite." She guided him into the bakery, closing the door behind them. After she locked it again, she drew the shade down over the window glass.

Dear heavens, what am I do to with him now?

His clothes, though wrinkled with a bit of blood staining them, were well-tailored and his shirt was of fine lawn, so he must be someone in the *beau monde*, which meant his title of Lord Frampton wasn't merely in jest for his boxing persona. Well, she had assumed since the announcer in the ring had called him that at the end of the round she'd watched. And the way he pronounced words spoke of the upper class.

Who was he, truly? Would someone come looking for him? Did he have a wife somewhere? That gave her pause as she assisted him up the narrow wooden stairs that led to the rooms above, but she was too far gone in the lie to stop now. If he'd *had* a wife, he wouldn't have come here alone, especially since he had entered a prize fight.

As soon as they entered the main room on the upper floor, she gestured him further into the room. "I'll help you clean your injuries, then I'll put some salve on them."

When his stomach rumbled, they both shared a laugh, though it was a bit strained. "I'm hungry. Can't remember when last I ate."

She nodded. "While you wash up, I'll prepare you a tray of cold cuts and such. After dinner, I'll read to you. Then we'll retire to bed." Heat slapped her cheeks at such forward behavior, and with a stranger to boot. "I'm sure the foreman will excuse your absence for a few days as your wound heals."

Especially since said person didn't exist.

"I suppose he will." He put a hand to his head. "My head aches like the devil."

"Go take care of ablations then. I'll fetch some water from downstairs." She gave him a little push toward the slightly larger of the two bedchambers. "I'll make you some willow bark tea with your tray of food while I'm down there. The tea will help with the pain." The more she spoke, the more excited she grew.

Could she finally be happy? And what about the villagers? They would ask questions, but she would tell them she married this man in secret, perhaps because there was a scandal and she *had* to. She might need to confide in her aunt to make things plausible. Hopefully, Aunt Bess wouldn't badger or chide too much.

If her luck held, he would retain the amnesia he suffered with for a little while yet. And by then, perhaps he would have contracted feelings for her.

"Thank you." He gave her a one-sided grin, probably due to the partially swollen lip. "Uh, this is embarrassing but I don't remember your name. It's not well done of me, since you are my wife."

A thrill twisted down her spine to be called that. "Oh, don't be embarrassed. I'm Phoebe, and I am so glad you're here with me."

Please forgive me.

Chapter Five

October 14, 1817
Bidwell's Bakery
Cranleigh, Surrey

I T HAD BEEN two days since William had stumbled to this bakery and was reunited with his wife. Though he couldn't remember anything about his life or what had happened to him to see him bloodied and battered past that night, he'd relied on Phoebe to help him fill in the details.

To be honest, recuperation in the cozy rooms above the bakery wasn't bad at all. His wife was a talented cook, and the foods that she brought him at various times throughout the day had left him quite satisfied. It was a simple life, and he hadn't been to his bricklayer position since he'd lost his memories; in fact, he didn't even know where to go or who to speak with about that. Though somehow it didn't matter, for he needed to heal from his injuries first.

One thing he'd discovered was that his wife was a dear little thing. While she worked downstairs in the bakery, he slept, or if he was awake, he would read from the few books he'd found in the rooms that were oddly devoid of decoration or anything that might have personal memories attached to it. In the evenings after her stint in the bakery was over, she'd come upstairs with his dinner, and they would share the meal together.

Phoebe—he'd had to ask her name again—was pretty in a fresh-faced, provincial way, and her blue eyes drew a man in without letting go. Petite, which put her a good several inches or so shorter than him, possessed curves that would tempt even the saints, and part of him was smug that she was his. And she smelled delightful, like summertime in the country amidst wildflower fields. As they'd readied for slumber last night, he'd caught her into his arms and kissed her, for he'd felt much better than he had the previous day. It was just a chaste kiss without much heat behind it, but then they'd laid down in the narrow bed together, but his wife had blushed as if she'd been an innocent schoolgirl. It was adorable, and gave him pause, for she was well past the first blush of youth, likely in her mid-twenties. Perhaps it didn't matter, and she was merely shy about such things, and if he was always away from home as she'd said, perhaps they didn't have time to show affection for each other.

Well, that is going to change.

Then Phoebe came into their shared bedchamber with her customary ready smile. "Aunt Bess has asked us to dinner tonight at her cottage. She says she has a hunter's stew that has been simmering all day long. With freshly baked bread, of course."

"I don't know what that is, but it sounds heavenly." He couldn't help but peer at her in the slightly cloudy mirror over the basin's table, for she'd stripped out of the day dress. When she moved to the clothespress clad in her unmentionables, he followed her with his gaze. "Uh, why does your aunt wish to have dinner with us?"

"She is worried about you, of course." When she glanced at him as she pulled a gown from the clothespress, there were shadows in her eyes, but why?

"Ah." Though he didn't remember meeting her from before, he looked forward to doing so tonight. "Do you wish for my assistance with the gown?" As he spoke, he came toward her, which was easy to do since the room wasn't that large. Seeing her with her petticoat and stays sent blood rushing to his member.

Where was the harm in tossing her onto their bed and having his way with her? To reacquaint himself with her plump curves?

"That would be lovely. Thank you." Again, there was a blush in her cheeks. Surely, she'd been clad in her underthings around him before. "Um, the gown is a few years out of date, but then, there hasn't been much cause for me—us—to be out in high society, so it doesn't matter."

Since he had no idea about their finances since he couldn't remember, if he discovered there was enough coin left over at month's end, he would buy her a new gown.

"Well, the copper color will be fantastic against your pale coloring and eyes." How had he been so fortunate as to win her? "Besides, it's quite autumnal."

"I do adore it." She struggled into the gown then presented him with her back. "You can do up the laces."

"Mmm." The second he drew his fingers over the taffeta, the tactile feel of it was so familiar that he'd swear he had done this before... only not with her. "Before you and I were married, was I involved with someone else?"

"Oh, I..." Her swallow was audible. "I'm not certain. You aren't originally from this area."

"Then where do I hail from?" Gently, he tightened the laces and tied them.

"London," she said in a hushed voice. "Apparently, living in Town was too expensive so you set out looking for work elsewhere, but close enough that you could easily access London if you wished."

"That makes sense. No doubt I'd want to remain close to family." Then the heat of her distracted him. He slipped his arms about her waist and pressed his lips to the crook of her shoulder. As she gave into a shiver, it transferred to him.

"No doubt," she said in a rather breathless voice. "But you are here now with me, and we have a good life."

"We do, but perhaps we should at least write to my family and inform them about my memory loss. If I could speak with them, see them in person, it might help."

"It might, of course, and it is something we can discuss," she said, yet there were shadows in the blue depths of her eyes, which had him wondering why.

Then he put the thoughts out of his mind. "There is one good thing about me losing my memory, though." William followed that by placing a soft kiss to the side of her neck.

"Oh? What's that?"

"We have the opportunity for a new honeymoon period, since I don't remember the first one, and I can have the fun of exploring you all over again."

"If you think it's necessary?"

"Of course it is. You are quite the temptation." Then, because he could, he turned her about, put a curled forefinger beneath her chin, raised her head, and fit his lips to hers. Damn but she felt good in his arms, and those two pillowy pieces of flesh tasted even better. Each movement he made over her mouth, she mirrored, and that slight hesitation there had the odd effect of lighting tiny fires in his blood. How was it that his wife could still retain the air of being an innocent? Eventually, he held her at arms' length while a bemused expression crossed her face. "We should finish our toilettes, else your aunt's dinner will be quite ruined."

Her eyes widened, and those impossibly blue pools threatened to pull him under. "Or I will be, hmm?" she asked in a soft voice.

That was rather odd, for hadn't she said they'd been married for six months? Surely, within that time frame they had lain together. William frowned. "I can easily arrange that if you'd like. No one would fault me by taking my wife to bed." And that led him to another odd thing. His body felt tight and strained, as if he desperately needed to break the tension building inside, but how was that possible? Hadn't he bedded his wife with regularity?

A blush stained her cheeks. "As lovely as that sounds, we should probably leave for Aunt Bess' cottage. She doesn't like it when her schedule is interrupted or delayed."

"I'll have to assume that's the truth since I don't remember, but I do look forward to having you to myself in the meanwhile." And perhaps he would have an opportunity this evening to question of the two of them. It was one thing to have lost his memories, but it was quite another to have answers that made sense.

A HALF HOUR later, William held out a chair for his wife at her aunt's dining table. It was a sturdy piece of furniture, oval in shape, that could seat six, and it was perfect for the three of them. What was more, Aunt Bess apparently didn't stand on ceremony, for instead of courses, the whole of the meal had been laid out on the table on platters, which made for a rustic appearance, and he for one heartily approved.

As the chicken was carved and passed around, Aunt Bess continued to shoot puzzled glances at him. Finally, once everyone had a full plate of food, he finally huffed out a breath, sat down, and then frowned.

"What is it you will say to me then, Aunt Bess? You continue to look at me as if you have a multitude of questions, but you never speak a word. So I'm curious. What is it about me that you find offensive or otherwise?" At least then he would know how to correct an issue if there was one.

Across from his location, Phoebe gasped. "William, for shame. She means no ill will."

Aunt Bess lifted a hand. A faint grin curved her lips. "He has every right to ask questions, dear. It must be difficult and quite frightening to know he had a life before and now can't remember any of it." For whatever reason, she narrowed her eyes at Phoebe. "We can only hope that if this amnesia is a permanent condition, he can make peace with it."

"Of course, Auntie. I just want him to be happy, no matter what." An odd air crackled between them, but William couldn't puzzle out why. "Haven't we both shown that his recent knock on the head hasn't changed anything between us? There has been no change in affection."

"Perhaps."

With a slight frown, William bounced his gaze between them. "Don't be at each other's throats because of me, ladies. I'll get better. You'll see."

"No doubt you will, and that is what I'm afraid of." After chewing and then swallowing a bit of chicken, Aunt Bess set down her fork. She landed all her focus on him. "It isn't that I don't like you, William, it is more of the fact that my niece essentially wished to run off with you and marry. I didn't want that to happen, so we had it arranged that you would marry in a quiet, private ceremony. It wasn't what I wanted for Phoebe, but she was quite demanding that the union be kept private."

He nodded. "I can understand that. However, wasn't that six months ago? Surely, any such animosity would have dissipated since then." Had he and her aunt been at odds before he lost his memories?

"To be honest, in the past few days, we've had no issue getting along." There was nothing except truth in her eyes. "However, I want to make certain you will treat my Phoebe right and that you will be kind to her. I don't wish anyone's heart to be broken on such an impulsive decision to… wed."

"Fair enough." Several moments of silence brewed in the room as the three of them tucked into their meal. "However, you have my word that I will never forsake your niece, or otherwise hurt her in any way. When I make a promise to someone, I keep it." He caught his wife's eye from across the table and grinned. "And just look at her. She's glowing, Auntie. How could I betray such a sweet woman? Especially after she has run herself ragged looking after me since my accident."

Another blush stained her cheeks. "You are so sweet, William," Phoebe murmured. "I haven't regretted for one moment our coming together."

Aunt Bess snorted. "I hope you'll still think that in a month or even a year, dear. There are times when I believe that some of your decisions have been *quite* desperate and they might come back to haunt you."

To Phoebe's credit, she showed a bit of backbone when she shook her head. "I am not worried about it, Aunt Bess. We will weather any storm together." One of her eyebrows rose in challenge. "Until then, there is no need to worry."

He didn't know what the tense undercurrent between the women meant, but he hoped it would eventually fade. "I appreciate your fierce defense of Phoebe. It's good that she has such a staunch supporter nearby." A ball of emotion lodged in his throat. "I'm glad she has you to lean on and talk to about my accident."

For a few seconds, confusion went through the older woman's eyes. Then she nodded. "Well, I need to be there for her since the whole of our family is now gone for various reasons, and the poor dear hasn't had much luck with fiancés in the past." She shrugged. "I suppose I'm grateful that you along when you did. Who knows what would have happened to her if you didn't." Her gaze was quite hawkish. "Do you promise to never leave her, no matter what happens in your future? Far too often, men change and decide they aren't happy with their choice of wives."

"Aunt Bess, I—"

The older woman waved a hand when Phoebe would have interrupted her. "I need to hear it from him."

What did it matter? Hadn't he already married the young woman? Pledged his life to her? But he sighed. Perhaps due to the family history of deaths and sadness, her aunt was a bit overly protective. "Of course I promise. Your niece and I are a pair. No matter what happens in the future, we will always be together. If trouble arises, not that I could ever think it will, I will stay by her side."

"I'm glad to hear you say that," Phoebe replied with a wide smile, as she bounced her gaze between the two of them. "Because I have some incredible news."

"Oh?" Immediately, more wariness than before jumped into Aunt Bess' expression. "I can't wait to hear *this*," she muttered.

Phoebe waved her comment away then landed her overly bright gaze on him. "I've just discovered I am with child."

The sudden clatter of silverware against china temporarily interrupted the conversation, for Aunt Bess had dropped her fork. "I beg your pardon?" The older woman stared with narrowed eyes at her niece. "You're certain?"

"Yes." Phoebe nodded, and her kissable lips curved into a pleased smile, although it didn't reflect in her eyes. "The midwife said nearly three months along."

Aunt Bess snorted. "How interesting, since you haven't yet exhibited any symptoms nor has your belly expanded."

Another blush stained Phoebe's cheeks. "No doubt all of that will come soon enough, but I *have* felt tired as of late. I thought it was just because I was worried about William's health." She turned her attention to him and when she smiled, he felt a pleasant sort of warmth that went through his chest. "I didn't want to mention this to you if it was merely a false alarm."

Another snort from Aunt Bess. "Or a figment of your imagination?"

They both ignored her this time.

William cleared his throat. He set his fork on his plate then tossed his napkin to the tabletop as he stood. After he came around the table, he went down on one knee at Phoebe's chair and took her hand. "We are to have a child together?"

"Yes." She shook her head. Tears welled in her blue eyes. "Are you happy?"

"I am, and I can hardly believe it." Knowing he would have a child helped to relieve the aches and pains that still lingered in his muscles.

"Neither can I," Aunt Bess said, apparently not caring that this was a tender moment between husband and wife.

"It is a blessed time, Auntie," William said to her, but he didn't release Phoebe's hand. "I'm damned glad I'm a bricklayer by profession, for perhaps we can expand the rooms above the bakery."

She nodded. "We can talk about that in the coming weeks."

Finally, he stood then leaned over her and pressed his lips to the top of her head. "I look forward to that, and everything else." As he resumed his chair, he glanced at his wife's aunt. "Isn't this amazing news, Auntie?"

"Oh, it's quite *something*, and I just hope hearts aren't broken at the end of it." She rested her gaze on Phoebe. "I have supported you in many things throughout your life, but there are times when I think that being under such a large amount of grief can warp a person's mind. Are you certain that isn't happening here?"

For a moment, tears welled in Phoebe's eyes. "Yes, I am certain that's not what this is." She threw a glance his way, but her smile was sad around the edges. "I'm so thankful you are here, William, and can't wait to see what else occurs in our lives."

He nodded. "I'll need to get my living again once my body is completely healed." It would make him feel better when he could provide for his family. "Or perhaps I should try my hand at something else, since apparently working with bricks is dangerous."

"It's definitely seemed that way for you from the moment you stepped foot in Cranleigh," Aunt Bess said, and then laughed when Phoebe glared at her. "For the moment, why we're keeping an eye on you, Phoebe can train you in working at the bakery. Might be good to keep the thing in the family once I'm off this mortal coil, and if you and Phoebe do it together? Even better."

Phoebe clapped her hands. "That would be such an amazing thing!" She glanced at him with large round eyes full of emotion. "Please say yes, William."

How could he deny such a plea? Then he nodded. "I'll give it a try, of course." It would be good to have a new challenge, for as much as his life was pleasant as it was, he couldn't help but feel there was something missing, something vital, yet he couldn't imagine what that was.

Chapter Six

October 15, 1817

"PHOEBE, A WORD, if you please."

Oh, dear.

There was a note of command in her aunt's voice that she would be a fool to ignore. "Of course, Aunt Bess." She wiped her hands on her pinafore apron, smiled at William, and nodded. "If a customer comes in, be your charming self and put their pastries in a box and take their coin. There is nothing complicated about it." When he acknowledged the request, she followed her aunt into the back room and then frowned as the older woman closed the door. "Is something amiss, Auntie?"

"You have the gall to ask me that?" her aunt questioned in a whispered hiss. She popped her hands on her hips as she stared. "After all the lies you've told in the past few days?"

Heat immediately went through Phoebe's cheeks. "I, uh—"

"And you with that smug smile every morning because you're living in sin with a stranger?" Slowly, her aunt shook her head. "And then putting forth the huge lie that you're with child? What the devil has come over you?"

The accusation was fair. "Do you want honesty or something that will make you feel better?" As she spoke, she drew her aunt toward the other side of the room so William—or whatever his real name was—wouldn't hear.

"I want the truth. You have been acting suspicious for days, and I'm quite concerned, especially after that farce of a dinner last night."

Hot guilt filled Phoebe's chest. "While I realize that, you have no idea how very lonely I am, Auntie." Tears rose in her eyes. "I have had far too much death and grief in my life, and I have lost two fiancés. And then suddenly, it seems that fate dropped this man into my lap who doesn't remember who he is. Why shouldn't I find a bit of happiness with him? Where is the harm?"

"Where is the harm?" Aunt Bess threw up an arm. "That man deserves better than to essentially be kidnapped by what I can only call desperation," she accused in an intense whisper. "What will you do if his memories come back and he realizes this isn't his life at all?"

"I guess I'll meet that challenge if—or when—it arises."

"And what are you going to say when the lie of your pregnancy makes itself known? You and I both know you aren't increasing, and I rather doubt he's bedded you in the few days he's been here, charming or not."

Another sweep of heat went through Phoebe's cheeks. "While it's true, he has not—for he hasn't felt quite the thing I'd imagine—we do share a bed. I needed to up the stakes in my story so he would, indeed, not leave me after you interrogated him last night." She shook her head. "I shall spin another tale if needed to explain away the absence of a swollen belly."

"Listen to yourself." Aunt Bess dropped her hands on Phoebe's shoulders and gave her a bit of a shake. "Almost every word out of your mouth is a lie."

"Can you blame me?" Phoebe said in a low-pitched hiss back to her. "My whole life has been a sad trial. Don't you think I deserve happiness? Perhaps even love?"

"Of course I do, but not this way." Aunt Bess' expression was like a thunderstorm. "You are committing crimes, dear. Kidnapping, for one. And what will you do if 'William's' family comes searching for him? They're going to discover where he is. Or worse, what if someone in the village or surrounding area recognizes your alleged husband? Tells him that he's a prize fighter? Your story is going to collapse around your feet."

"I don't know." It was the first honest thing she'd said in a few days. "I'm hoping that it won't matter because he'll have fallen in love with me by then."

"That is much to ask of fate, especially when you're involving a man." There was a look of incredulity in her aunt's eyes. "Is he truly a lord?"

Phoebe nodded. "That is what the announcer at the bout referred to him as, so I assume he's a member of the *beau monde*."

"That is even worse." A trace of panic went through Aunt Bess' eyes. "I wouldn't be surprised if his family, once they notice he's missing, sends out a man from Bow Street to hunt him down."

Knots of worry pulled in Phoebe's belly. "Do you truly think that will happen?"

"Well, obviously, he'll be missed. The question remains when will your false marriage come to a halt?" One of Aunt Bess' eyebrows rose in inquiry. "And then, if he seduces you—or rather you do the same to him—and he does bed you, what if you're left with a babe in your belly and his family takes him back to London? He'll forget all about you once he returns to his previous—and rightful—life. And you'll be left ruined, in scandal and tears."

"I suppose I'd hoped that wouldn't come 'round so soon." For the first time since this odyssey began did Phoebe think about the consequences of her actions. "I am enjoying spending time with him, though. He's interesting in his own right, but truth to tell, it's exhausting to always need to invent a story for his history."

"You wouldn't need to do that if you'd done things the right way."

"Oh, Auntie, the last thing I need right now is a lecture." Suddenly, a wave of exhaustion went through Phoebe. "I just want romance in my life, I want a man to call my own who will love me, and to find whatever joy we can have together. Is that too much to ask?"

"No, it's not, but when you do it this way, folks will call you slightly demented." Her aunt took a deep breath then let it ease out. "I don't want my friends or customers thinking that of you or assuming you are a criminal, and I certainly don't want the authorities to haul you away to an asylum. Above everything, I don't want to see your heart broken again, and this time it won't be due to death." She patted Phoebe's cheek. "If you fall in love with this man and he goes back to previous life—because why wouldn't he; he'd never asked to be here—you will once more be alone, and it'll be much worse this time."

For a long moment, she considered her aunt's words. Then she nodded. "Thank you for looking out for me and being protective. I'll be careful. I promise."

Aunt Bess huffed. "So then, you won't tell him the truth?"

"Not right now."

"You know, when it comes out—and it will—it should come from you first. He might trust you now, but once that is broken, it will be entirely too difficult to regain."

She nodded. "I'll bear that in mind." But for now, she was enjoying this newfound freedom far too much.

"And by the by, how the hell are you explaining to him his lack of wardrobe? I've seen you sneaking your belongings from the cottage to the rooms you're currently living in, but what about his things? Shaving kit, boots, all the rest?" One of her aunt's eyebrows rose in question.

"Very carefully." Phoebe huffed in frustration. "I picked up a shaving set at the pawn shop, along with a worn pair of boots. And there were a few of Charles' things I had tucked in my trunk that fit William." Certainly, her brother wouldn't mind since he'd perished in the war. "Then I bought a few pieces from the modiste that had been commissions someone didn't wish to have after they were completed."

"And he hasn't questioned why his wardrobe is mismatched and lacking?"

"Not that I know of. If he's complained, it hasn't been to me."

Aunt Bess shook her head. "If you are intent in doing this, I'll dig through some of your father's possessions I'd packed away after his death. He was about the same size as your pretend husband, so at least he'll not be lacking."

She nearly wilted with relief. "Thank you for your support."

"And I'll be there for you when this all falls apart," Aunt Bess said as she walked toward the door. "Let us hope that doesn't happen for a while yet."

Amen to that.

Later that afternoon

PHOEBE WAS ELATED that William wished to go on a stroll with her through the country lanes and meadows. They'd even taken a picnic basket with them to have tea alfresco later if they could find a shady spot. After the far too honest talk with her aunt earlier that morning, her mind was conflicted about what to do about telling her false husband the truth. It wouldn't help to say anything right now, for she didn't know who his people were, and didn't know anything about him other than his title was Lord Frampton.

Could she put him on the post coach to London with only that information and wish him luck in finding his family? Of course, but how frightening would that be? Even for a man, and she didn't have the heart to do that.

"You seem as if you are a million miles away," William said as he touched her hand with his. "Is all well? Are you feeling poorly?"

Oh, dear.

"I'm well enough, thank you." She turned her head so she

could see him past the shallow brim of her simple straw bonnet. "Woolgathering, I suppose."

"It's only natural that your thoughts might turn inward during this time. No doubt it's a bit intimidating being in the family way."

"Yes." The response was quite breathless, for if she wasn't careful, she'd blurt out the truth. "But for now, I'm doing well, so I plan to enjoy the walk in the fresh air."

He nodded. "In your condition, you shouldn't be on your feet for all those hours in the bakery. Should I ask your aunt to either give you a stool or get on without you for a few hours?"

Dear heavens, that will mean another lecture from Aunt Bess.

"I wouldn't. When the time comes, I'll speak with her. I'm sure she'll understand, but I'm not an invalid, so please don't treat me as if I were." She frowned. Was that what he was doing, or was it simply kindness?

"Of course you're not." William took her hand and pulled her closer to him. "I'm merely trying to protect you and the babe." He winked. "It's quite an exciting prospect, knowing I'll be a father in half a year."

Emotions lodged in her throat, for it was all a lie. None of what she'd told him was real; their relationship wasn't real, yet the feeling of security she had each time she laid down next to him in the narrow bed was. As was the sensation of happiness whenever he kissed her. "It is certainly interesting to contemplate."

They walked in silence for a bit on the country lane that led away from the village.

"Tell me about you," he said abruptly, breaking the companionable quiet.

"What do you mean?" The knots of worry in her belly pulled once more.

William shrugged. "I can't remember anything about you or our history together, so since we're having a romantic walk, I thought it might be lovely to get to know you, as if I'm courting you all over again."

A flutter went around her heart. "What a good idea." How would he have courted her to begin with? Of course, that assumed a man like him who have ever picked her out of a crowd for such an intention. They would never move in the same circles in reality.

"I thought so." Amusement twinkled in his light brown eyes, and the grin that curved his sensual lips sent matching flutters through her lower belly. "How did you and I meet?"

It would seem there was even more lying in her immediate future. If there came a time for the truth, would he be as enamored with her as he seemed to be now? Afraid of knowing the answer, Phoebe softly cleared her throat. "Uh, Auntie and I were up in London last year for the Christmastide season and to take in the sights. We happened to attend the same rout where you were at, and I accidentally bumped into you, spilling a bit of Maderia on your tailcoat." It was entirely plausible, because being in society made her extremely nervous.

"I trust I wasn't an arse in my reaction."

She chuckled. "Not completely, but you weren't pleased." If she were to invent a meeting, it might as well amuse her. "You were charming, however, and when I asked how I could make it up to you, a dance was your answer."

"That sounds about right. I think." When he laughed, the warm, rich tones of the sound sent shivers down her spine. "But I wish I would have remembered what it felt like to dance with you."

"Oh? Do you enjoy that exercise?"

He shrugged. "Your guess is as good as mine, but somehow, I feel like I might. Don't you enjoy it?"

"I do, but here in Cranleigh, there aren't many opportunities unless the assembly rooms are open or there is a private event a someone's country home." The solid feel of his body at her side was quite thrilling, and made her remember how much she missed her fiancés. In William, though, she'd found an easy companionship and a vibrant partner she could envision spending time with in the future.

If fate would allow it.

"Clearly, you need to use your imagination, love. Dancing doesn't need any of that and can take the exercise in any flat place. Take that meadow, in fact. Do you fancy a waltz?"

Her pulse accelerated. "Perhaps another time."

"Fair enough." He nodded. "Have you always lived in Cranleigh?"

"I have. My parents were both born here, as were me and my siblings."

"And yet you lost all of them, I assume?"

Swallowing heavily, Phoebe nodded. "Either through the war or another of fate's cutting of threads. Life hasn't been kind, I'm afraid." Then she shrugged. "Before you came along, I'd been engaged to two men, and both perished. I had given up hope of ever finding anyone again."

"I'm sorry to hear that, but I'm glad to be here for you." When he squeezed her fingers, tears welled in her eyes. "You have told me that my family lives in London. Do they regularly come to visit?"

"They haven't come for ages, probably because they don't think I'm good enough for you." That wouldn't be far from the truth if his memory returned and he went back to the life he'd led before in Town.

"Then they are idiots, for you are everything lovely in this world, and I couldn't imagine going through life with anyone else at my side."

The words were sweet and romantic, of course, but she doubted he truly meant them, for he only thought himself in love with her because she'd told him they were married. Why couldn't this life become real? Then she paid attention to their location and sucked in a breath.

Immediately on alert, he tugged her to a halt. "What?"

"Nothing, really, but see that meadow?" She pointed to the

space where she'd first seen him on the day of the fight. "Sometimes, they hold bare knuckle boxing matches there."

"How interesting." He released her hand and then wandered off the lane toward the meadow, while she followed at a slower pace. "Bare knuckle boxing." With a glance at her over his shoulder, William moved into the meadow. "I'll wager those attract large crowds, hmm?"

"So they say. I attended one for only a quarter of an hour, and even then, I had on a cloak, so I'd be partially hidden." An image of him shirtless and stripped to his breeches floated into her mind. "No doubt it's a brutal sport."

"So I've heard." He swept his gaze over the long, sweet-smelling grasses and flowers. "I would have enjoyed watching that." The hand not holding the basket curled into a fist. "I've heard a few people talking about such things in passing and can only imagine how thrilling a raw sport like that is."

"Have you ever seen a bout before?" she asked, as she drew abreast of him.

"Obviously, I don't remember if I did."

"Yet you said something about a Young Thomas to me before."

Confusion reflected in his eyes. "I don't remember saying that, but something about those words is familiar to me." The man glanced at her with a slight smile. "I can almost understand what it feels like to land a punch into another's man's gut, to know the rush of satisfaction of clipping some man's chin with a fast uppercut."

How did he know the language? Did that mean he was remembering? He'd certainly been bloodied and battered when he'd come stumbling out to the bakery, and that mean he'd probably come straight from this very meadow after his bout. But seeing him cleaned up and fully clothed now instead of half-naked was a far sight better than the mess he'd been.

"Just make sure you don't go around the village picking fights, hmm?"

"Of course I won't, especially with a child on the way." Then he took her hand once more and pulled her away from the meadow. "Even if I had the skill, fighting for coin is a risk. Each man only has half a chance of winning, but both have every chance of being seriously injured enough that it would affect their daily lives."

At a grouping of oak trees, he found a spot he liked then sat with his back against the trunk of a wide tree with his legs encased in tight-fitting trousers in a brown color stretched out in front of him. Once he rested the basket beside him, William gestured to her, patted his lap. "Come. I'm of a mood to spend some scandalous time with my wife."

"Oh?" Tingles zipped up and down her spine, but when he lifted an eyebrow, there was nowhere else to go except to join him. "What... uh, what do you have in mind?" This could either go very, very good or very, very wrong.

"Come closer and we'll find out together." He tapped the basket's lid. "And I brought a Gothic novel I found shoved in between the cushions of the sofa in our common room. I don't mind reading you a couple of chapters if that is the sort of literature you enjoy."

Good heavens. She must have left that book behind years ago when she'd visited her aunt before all the grief entered her life. "Sounds intriguing." And why shouldn't she explore this man? She'd invented a marriage, didn't she? And if was already in the midst of scandal, she might as well enjoy it. With a grin, Phoebe took her skirts in hand and crawled over to his location. "What made you bring the book?"

He shrugged as he removed his gloves, then threw them toward the basket. "I took a chance, thinking the book might belong to you, one that you didn't want your aunt to know you liked to read." One hand rested on the lid of the picnic basket. "In case you think your aunt has no knowledge of this outing, it was on her suggestion I bring the basket. She packed it herself, said I should go flirt with my wife. There is even a carafe of tea, though

I rather doubt it has retained its warmth, but even cold tea is preferable to none."

"What a lovely idea." Needing to see where this interlude would lead, Phoebe climbed into his lap, straddling him with her skirts bunched between them. Dear heavens, the feelings that welled within her from this wicked position caught her by surprise. "Oh!"

"Ha. I knew you weren't immune to my advances, so it must be your aunt's censure you're trying to mitigate for some reason." Immediately, his arms went around her, and daring much, she relieved him of his top hat, tossing it to the side. "Why are you at odds with her? I know you argued with her this morning, even though I couldn't hear what you talked about."

Heat went through Phoebe's cheeks. "I don't wish to discuss that." How could she even form words when she was pressed so intimately against him?

"Fair enough." William nodded. "Then if you don't want to talk, would you like to make inroads into tea?"

"Not just yet." When she met his gaze, she nearly tumbled into those darkening brown depths. In the sunlight, and this close to him, she discerned tiny golden flecks in those pools. "This is hardly proper, though it feels all too good." Would he laugh at her for the admission?

He chuckled. "Proper is far too overrated," he murmured and slipped a hand up her spine to tangle in her hair. "And I can't explain to you why I feel as if I was a rogue at one time."

"Mmm, perhaps you were, for you are certainly quite charming." This time, she initiated the kiss between them, and all too soon the embrace grew heated. How could it not when there was a strong connection there even if he was much a stranger? Without knowing exactly what she was doing, Phoebe plundered his mouth, sought out his tongue with hers, for that tangle of tongues, the exchanging of thrusts that he'd taught her was a sensation she craved.

William broke the kiss to drag his lips down the side of her neck. When he followed the simple line of her bodice, she trembled in his hold, and with a smug chuckle, he took one of her taut nipples into his mouth and worried it through the thin fabric of her dress. The other he rubbed and rolled until her back arched and she writhed from his erotic attentions.

Dear heavens.

She never felt as if she might explode before, since both of her fiancés had been away to war, and their few meetings hadn't been conducted by themselves. And thank goodness her dress was of a lightweight wool blend so no one would see the wetness his mouth left behind. "Oh, goodness," she managed to gasp out as her head lolled onto one shoulder. The evidence of his desire rubbed against her center, and it was a marvelous feeling. Would she be able to see his member soon?

"You have no idea how much I want you, but this isn't the time or place." Yet he delved a hand beneath her skirting and seconds later, those questing fingers were between her splayed thighs to play at the sensitive button at her center.

"Dear heavens, what are you doing?" Not of her own volition, her fingers dug into his shoulders.

"The next best thing Mrs...." He frowned. "Damn. I can't remember my surname."

Fear twisted down her spine, for she'd forgotten that within her network of lies. "Harris," she managed to force out from a tight throat. "William Harris."

"Of course. That sounds right." A chuckle left his throat when she uttered a moan mixed with a sigh and one of her hands slipped down his chest. "And to answer your question, I'm pleasuring my wife, so you can be as loud as you wish."

"Oh." *I'm in a fair amount of trouble, I think.* Confused about what to do, Phoebe claimed his mouth in a hard kiss while he continued to tease that nubbin for all he was worth. The strum of his fingers against the sensitive flesh had the power to see her undone, and she rather liked it. "William..."

"Shh. Give into the feelings, Phoebe."

"But…" How? But her body took control, and instinctively, she moved against his fingers and hand, which put her into his keeping much better. At the new angle, it took next to no time for her to fall over the edge into bliss with a sound that was halfway between a cry and a scream. Did it speak to his skill that she'd achieved that so quickly? As waves of hot sensation rushed over her, she squirmed on his lap, moved her hips against his hand. He was only too happy to oblige her and continued to bedevil that button until she lost the last vestiges of control and went over again. Exhausted, Phoebe sagged into his chest, and as his arms once more went around her, he held her close. "Merciful heavens. That was… There are no words."

"Have you never achieved release in all the times we've been together?" Confusion threaded through his voice as it rumbled in her ear.

"Yes, of course, but this time was particularly powerful." How was she to remember her lies when his play could make her forget everything? As her heartbeat regulated, she nestled herself against his chest and sighed. For the first time in her life, she'd been sent flying, and what was more, she couldn't wait to experience that again.

"Then I must be doing something right." He pressed his lips to her temple. "Now, let us investigate the contents of that basket. I'm famished."

Was it horrid of her to pray that his memories never returned?

Chapter Seven

October 16, 1817

WILLIAM PAUSED TO wipe his brow, for he'd gone out to a wooded area in order to chop firewood. Last night, the weather had changed, and it had brought with it a bit of a cold snap, one where his breath clouded about his head in the mornings and evenings. And it was chilly in the cozy apartment above the bakery.

Couldn't have the mother of his unborn child feeling cold.

After he'd chopped the final log, he piled the split pieces into a large burlap bag then took up both that and the axe and headed back toward the business district of the village. The sun had set about an hour ago, and when he'd left, Phoebe hadn't yet come upstairs from her duties at the bakery. But now the temperatures had dropped, and he wanted nothing more than to sit in their common room with the fire cheerfully burning behind the plain iron grate and Phoebe in his arms.

As he approached one of the taverns, a man came out of that establishment and nearly careened into William, but quickly corrected himself.

"My apologies." The tall man touched the brim of his beaver felt top hat. Then he peered closer. "Are you that Stapleton man, the bare-knuckle boxer who fought here a week ago?"

William frowned. "I am not. Merely William Harris."

"Ah." The other man nodded. "You have the look of 'im, but then, I suppose anyone would in the dark."

"Did you, ah, attend the bout?"

"I did! It was a long one, and the fighters were well-matched. Damn, but I always wager on a Stapleton brother if they're in the ring."

"Why? I'm not sure I've heard that name." But then, if he had, he wouldn't have remembered it.

"All the Stapleton brothers are the sons of the legendary George Stapleton, one of the best boxers in the history of the sport. They always put on a good show." The other man curled his hands into fists and mimicked a few movements. "Too damn bad Duncan Stapleton, or rather Lord Frampton as he's known in the *ton*, lost the last bout. Gossip holds he disappeared after that fight, too embarrassed to show his face in society again."

"He must have lost the match horrifically then." William settled the back of split logs more comfortably on his shoulder.

"Oh, he did. Went down hard in the last round. I couldn't believe it."

He nodded. "I can't imagine what that must have felt like." Except, for some odd reason, talking about boxing seemed familiar, as if he were knowledgeable regarding it at some point in his past. As he stood chatting with the other man, the names for movements filtered into his mind, as did the importance of quick footwork.

What the devil did that mean?

"Me neither, and bare-knuckle fighting is quite the talent." The other man nodded to William as he passed. "Next time a bout comes to Cranleigh, you should attend. There is something primal about watching two men beat the hell out of each other for nothing more than bragging rights and the roar of the crowd."

In his head, that exact sound filled his ears as if he were intimately acquainted with just that. *What is happening to me?* "I'll definitely consider it. Thank you, friend." Then he continued along the streets until he reached the bakery. Using his key, he let himself in, locked the door behind him, and went up the narrow wooden stairs to the rooms he shared with his wife.

"Is that you, William?" she called from the bedchamber they shared.

"Yes. Brought in some wood for the fire. The chill in the air is heralding perhaps an early winter." So saying, he dropped the bag of logs next to the small hearth. "Shall I build up the fire or would you prefer to snuggle beneath blankets?"

"Hmm. There is no doubt a way we can stay warm while in bed, don't you think?"

Did that mean she was amenable to physical relations to-night? "I do."

Phoebe came into the common room as she tied the sash of a thin lawn wrapper that matched her ivory night dress. Both garments were well-worn but still pretty and feminine, and they clung to her curves, for her skin was slightly damp. "Thank you for filling the bathtub for me before you went out."

"You're welcome." Damn, but he nearly forgot how to form words as he raked his gaze over her luscious form. The bathtub she spoke of was half a barrel used for either molasses or whiskey. No doubt they couldn't afford a porcelain tub or even one of brass, but it was a simple pleasure his wife enjoyed a couple times a week. When she came home from the bakery, she was usually exhausted and drained. "You shouldn't be on your feet so long in your condition."

"Don't fuss so." There was a blush in her cheeks as she crossed the room toward him. "It's early days yet. All is well."

"Good." As he removed his greatcoat—Phoebe had told him they'd bought it second hand from a gentleman who needed to cover debts—he watched her as she prowled over the floor. Those damp curves, the way the thin nightclothes clung to her frame, bewitched his mind, and in the light of the fire and the few lit candles, she was luscious and tempting.

And, God help him, he wanted her. It was as natural as breathing. This feeling, this desire, he remembered. It came up through the murky and shadowy depths of his broken brain, but he knew he'd bedded women before. Of course one of them was his wife; why else as she with child? It was time to indulge in that exercise again now that his bumps and bruises were well on the way to healing.

"Is that all you would say, Mr. Harris?" she asked with amusement threading through her dulcet tones.

"No, but I don't want to spook you." Needing something to occupy his mind lest he give into his urges and take her on the low table like an animal, William took her hand and pulled her into the bedchamber they shared.

"I rather doubt anything you could say or do would do that. Haven't we been married for months, and have known each other for even longer?"

"I will take your word for it." As soon as he skirted around the bathtub, he brought her over to the cheval glass. It had a few cloudy spots, but most of the glass was still usable. "On my way home, I spoke with a fellow who talked about bare-knuckle boxing. Said I put him in mind of a boxer."

"Oh?" A guarded expression flitted over her face. "Why did he think so?"

"I have no idea." He shrugged. "Perhaps I have one of those faces, but it got me to thinking about boxing and how familiar it seems to me."

"Well, you might have enjoyed watching bouts before you and I got together."

"That could be it." But he couldn't shake the feeling that it was more of that. As if boxing had meant something deeper to him at one time. Not knowing, he held her close. "How was I fortunate enough to land a woman as beautiful as you?" he whispered with his lips against the shell of her ear as he peered into the glass, meeting her gaze there.

"No doubt it will remain a mystery." Though she smiled at him, shadows clouded her eyes, and he couldn't puzzle out why. "Let us just say it was fate."

He slipped his arms about her waist then pulled her backside flush against his front. "If you had to do it all over again, would you?"

Would he?

"Of course." She dropped her gaze and rested her hands over his. "You are the first man in my life who hasn't disappointed me." A waver set up in her voice. "And you haven't left me as the rest of my family has, so yes, I would make the same decisions that I did which led me to you."

That was an odd admission, but he supposed he couldn't fault her for that. "Perhaps in time, we can make the bakery more profitable than it currently is, and when your aunt decides to retire, we will have the coin to buy our own cottage or perhaps even take a trip to Brighton." Above all, he wanted to give his wife everything that she deserved.

"I would like that very much." A sigh escaped her. "Do you ever dream of being someone else, someone more successful or high in society?"

"I haven't recently, but I can't speak to the rest of my life that I can't remember." Needing to see more of her body, William manipulated the sash of her robe, and when it gaped open, he encouraged it down her arms and torso, and then finally off her form. A groan rose in his throat, for the outline of her hardened nipples was evident behind her damp and clinging night dress. "And what would I do if I were a gentleman about Town? Don't I have all that I need here in Cranleigh?"

"I hope you do and that you truly believe that." She leaned back against him and raised a hand to cup his cheek. "We have a happy life even if we aren't excessively wealthy or titled as the members of the *beau monde* are."

"One doesn't need all of that to enjoy what they have." Quickly, he turned her about in his arms, pulled her close, and kissed her. Ah, yes, her lips, the warmth of her, the floral scent of her was definitely familiar. "How often do you and I share intimacy?" he asked, and with every word, his lips brushed hers.

She fiddled with the buttons on his jacket as a blush stained her cheeks. "As often as we need to, but I especially adored what you did to me beneath the oak trees."

"Ah. Then I'll be certain to give you a repeat performance." He briefly cupped her cheek. It was far too obvious they needed to chase carnal activities more often. "Would you like that?"

"Oh, yes." Her eyes sparkled as if they were gemstones in the sun. "But I want to explore you as well."

The words sent gooseflesh sailing over his skin. "I'm sure we can arrange that." With a grin, William tugged the pins from the loose bun she'd done with her hair to keep it out of the bath water. They clattered upon the floor with soft *pings*. "I want to show you how much you mean to me." Because that was what he felt for her, wasn't it?

"Oh!" Her eyes widened. "You have feelings for me?"

"Of course, silly widgeon. Why wouldn't I?" He stepped away long enough to divest himself of his boots and clothing. Soon the hardwood was littered with his garments and hers, for he couldn't wait any longer to see her nude... and actually remember it this time. "I don't know why you chose me when you could have attracted someone much better." He stood behind her once more, cupping her breasts, watching her in the cheval glass.

When she smiled, his world tipped sideways, and he fell into the sapphire depths of her eyes. "You were the one that I wanted." She shivered as he rolled her nipples. "There is nothing more to say." Nothing but honesty rang in her voice.

"I'm damned flattered, and hope I live up to your expectations, even if we *have* been married for six months." How cruel fate was to take that time away from him, for he didn't remember how she'd looked on their wedding day or the soft sounds she'd made when he'd first taken her to bed. "But I mean to make the most of the time we have left together, come what may."

She glanced sharply at him in the cheval glass. "Why would you say that?"

"What?" He shrugged, confused at why she was suddenly so upset. "I only meant that the days aren't guaranteed, and we don't know how long our service upon this earth will be."

"Oh." When she nodded, his muscles relaxed. "That makes more sense."

"Than what?"

Phoebe shook her head. "It's not important."

"Good, but if you don't mind, I don't wish to talk any longer." And there was no need. Everything he had to say could be accomplished by touch, by caress... by the act of coupling.

"Meaning... oh!"

The warmth of her beneath his hands was as comforting as his favorite pair of gloves, and the silkiness of her skin pushed him to the borders of madness. William nuzzled the crook of her shoulder as he teased her breasts, plucked at her nipples, and rolled them from root to tip. God, her body could tempt a saint, and he meant to explore every centimeter of it tonight. When she trembled and pressed one of his hands to her breast, he chuckled.

"If you think for a second that I would stray from all you represent, you are indeed a silly goose."

She giggled. "Do shut up, Mr. Harris."

"Ha." William walked her over to the bed and gently tumbled them onto it, where he spent copious minutes learning every inch of her body with his fingers, tongue, and lips. And those precious moments meant delight for them both.

Every moan and gasp she made went straight to his stones, but he continued to usher her closer to the edge of pleasure. The faint scents of lavender filled his nose, reminding him of the bar of soap she favored. Perhaps he should save up some coin to purchase a bottle of fancy perfume for her this coming Christmastide. A very faint taste of that flower came away on his tongue, but the fresh taste of her skin added a comforting sense to his play. Phoebe writhed beneath him as if everything he treated her to was new or that she hadn't expected it. That alone was a great aphrodisiac. Each time she reached for him, he batted her hands away, for he wasn't nearly done worshipping her.

"Let me touch you," she said, with a slight whine to her voice.

"Later."

"But that's not… fair!" Her voice rose from his ministrations.

With a chuckle, he kissed and suckled her breasts, teased her nipples with his tongue until she arched her back and begged him to leave off. But he wanted—needed—to see her spend; it was as vital to him as breathing, so he slipped a hand between her thighs and encouraged the tiny bundle of nerves from hiding. He manipulated that bud, that center of her pleasure, to within an inch of its life, applying various degrees of friction until he found what she enjoyed most. When she cried out, tumbling over the edge of a gentle, cresting release, he grinned against her soft skin. Not nearly done, he nibbled a path between her breasts and down her torso, lifting her hips as he went. When he buried his head between her thighs, licking the place he'd touched with his fingers, a curious sound of a moan mixed with a scream issued from her.

"William, stop!" The urgency of her whisper only pushed him to continue. "Such scandal this is."

"There is no one around to witness the act, and besides, we are married. Where is the harm?" He chuckled when she pressed her fingertips to her lips in an effort to quell the sound. "Let me play." Then he resumed the exquisite torture designed to send her flying a second time.

Which she did in short order. Despite her attempt to stem her response, the muffled scream sent pleasure directly into his engorged length. A flush appeared on her chest and cheeks, a sure sign he'd worked her properly over. As she went pliant on the bed, he took possession of her mouth once more, and as she returned the overture, it was him who experienced the feeling of falling.

Everything he did to her on that bed felt new and fresh, as if he were chasing that high for the first time with her, but he didn't think anything of it, for that was how the whole of his interactions with her had been. Perhaps a result of his injuries that had stolen his memories, but that only meant he was treated to the joys of putting her through her paces all over again, of learning the secrets of her body that would make her scream.

And he couldn't have enough.

"William, please…" When she found his gaze with hers, there was a hunger in those blue pools that matched his own. "I need you inside me." She held his head between her palms so she could direct his attention. "If that doesn't happen soon, I am liable to perish."

"You won't perish, sweeting." He grinned even as his hardened length pulsed with the same sort of urgency she exhibited. "But I understand the need." But first, he would kiss her until she couldn't remember her own name.

Chapter Eight

P HOEBE'S WORLD WENT tip over tail and continued to pinwheel into pleasure and sensations she'd never experienced before.

Since he'd sent her flying in the meadow, she'd craved more of that attention. After her bath tonight, she made the decision with herself that she wanted her false marriage with William—or whatever his name was—to be a union in every way that mattered. It didn't matter that they weren't married or had never spoken vows to each other. In countless tiny ways, each day that went by, he showed himself to be a kind, caring, charming man that any woman would be grateful to have landed.

Then she'd been caught up in his kisses, and now that he was naked, would he let her explore? Heat went over her person as she shoved at his shoulder until he lifted slightly off her body. "I want to touch you, kiss you all over as you've done to me." She drew a hand down his chest and reveled in the light sprinkling of brown hair found there. "Before I go insane from what you're doing to me."

His grin was a thing of beauty. "After we finish coupling." When she pouted, he chuckled, and the warmth of his breath skated over her cheek. "There is only so long I can postpone my urges, and already my control is fraying because I want to join with you so damned much."

"Oh!" Though it was the height of vulgar, it was also romantic, and flutters went through her lower belly. "All right." Surely, she would certainly go to hell for this. They weren't really married, and all her lies were horrible. There was no excuse for what she'd done, merely because she was lonely and wanted to find happiness in any way she could. Now, she was about to share the ultimate intimacy with him, and she had no idea what to do. "I want that too."

"Good." He brought his mouth crashing down on hers, and she had the distinct feeling that he was done talking. That kiss was fierce and intense; she felt it through every nerve ending. Something was exchanged between them in those lovely seconds where their souls had connected. Had he felt it too? When he was done, and her limbs had the strength of cooked porridge, he pulled slightly away to rest his forehead against hers. "Since I have no idea of what occurred between us the past six month because those memories have been stolen from me, I feel compelled to say these words to you now."

"Oh?" She couldn't help the trembles that played her spine.

"I love you. The welcome you give to me, the way you care for me, the way you have looked after me when I came home battered and bloodied. Youhave shown me how damned grateful I am that I managed to win you instead of losing you to another man."

Oh, dear heavens!

Was this part of the lie, or was he truly honest? It must be, for he had nothing to gain from dissembling, while she had everything to lose. Tears filled her eyes, and for the first time since this journey began, she knew this was where she was meant to be. And with him. "That's all I've ever wanted. A man of my own, who loves me with no restrictions."

Would it always be this way?

"I vow to keep growing so our union will flourish, because I cannot imagine a life where you aren't there. We are good for each other." This time he treated her to deep, drugging kisses that fused their souls.

Phoebe clung to him. Was she falling in love with this man? It was difficult to say since the new sensations confused her, and she was constantly worried that his memories would come back, bringing anger and shock. And perhaps she couldn't let herself fall for fear he'd leave her for his original life. But right now, in this moment, she looped her arms about the wide breadth of his shoulders and pressed herself into him. When he enfolded her into his embrace, flutters danced through her lower belly and throbs of need went through her. It was maddeningly how much she wanted this man—her pretend husband—but she would go out of her mind if he didn't claim her.

Finally she would know what it felt like to couple with him.

He must have known the direction of her thoughts, or perhaps he saw it in her expression, for he slid his hands down her body to grasp her hips and pulled her so close to his body that the insistent hardness of his shaft pressed into her belly. William made love to her mouth as if he'd thought of nothing except that for the last few days.

Oh, this feeling of safety and belonging was so lovely! She danced her fingertips along his chest, followed the contours and dips, traced a few of the scars before letting a hand drift to that part of him she had been curious about from the start.

He groaned when she cupped his equipage, gasped as she stroked her hand up and down that length, but he didn't bid her nay as he continued to kiss her, and with every thrust and parry of his tongue to hers, the more heat encompassed her, and need threatened to carry her away.

As she wrapped her fingers around his shaft, he cupped her breasts, kneaded them, worried the nipples into aching, pebbled buds with his thumbs. There was so much about his body she wished to explore. Her concentration fled the longer he teased her breasts and completely died the second he sucked one of the tips into his mouth. "You would do this again? I thought we would couple…"

"Oh, we will, but perhaps I wish to tease you a bit more before claiming you," he said between kisses and suckling. "Allow me this treat, for we haven't done this since my incident."

"While that is true, I'm going out of my mind with want." Had she captured a tiger by his tail by allowing him access to her body? But then, it was her lies that put them together, so she might as well enjoy it.

"Then I'm doing it right." He lightly bit her lower lip. "Wrap your legs around my waist."

She'd barely followed his instructions before he put a hand between her thighs. A cry left her throat the second he found that tiny bundle of nerves. Anticipation shallowed her breath. Another sound of pleasure echoed in the room when he teased her with various levels of friction.

Mercy, how could she survive another onslaught of exquisite torture?

A haze of passion clouded her mind. She pressed her lips to as many places on his person as she could reach. He was so hard and firm, and the muscles he possessed made her curious. Eventually, she would map his form with her tongue, but in this moment, she could barely concentrate while he rubbed her swollen nubbin. Already primed, a tiny scream escaped her throat as she shattered in his arms. A rush of pleasure hurtled her over the edge once more into a world that only existed in joy and the most wonderous sensations imaginable. Intense flutters rocked her.

"Never will I tire of watching you find bliss." William chuckled as if he'd wished for that reaction the whole time they'd been together. "Ah, Phoebe." Before the residual tremors from her release faded, he penetrated her body, not stopping until he'd fully seated himself.

The sharp prick of pain as he broke through her maidenhead surprised her. When she gasped, she strove to hide the fact she was, indeed, an innocent and not the pregnant wife he thought. Needing to distract him, she nibbled a spot beneath his jaw that he apparently favored. "Dear heavens," she whispered against his skin. "You are so large." Being impaled on his thick, hot length was one of the best things she'd ever experienced.

"Are you well? I haven't harmed the babe?" Concern threaded through his voice as he paused and searched out her gaze.

Heat slapped at her cheeks from the lie. "Don't worry," she whispered. "All is well." And she wriggled into a more comfortable position as she gripped his shoulders.

Then there were no words. They communed in a dance as old as time itself. Again and again, he speared into her, his powerful hips flexing, and each time she was pressed into the mattress, doing nothing except receiving him, welcoming him, giving herself to her false husband and taking what she needed from him. Deeper he went, touching her soul perhaps, and she dug her fingernails into his shoulders, for with each push, shivery sensation washed over her.

This was the most wonderful moment of her life, and just now, she had no regrets in fooling this man.

Then his rhythm changed. His thrusts become more frantic, fast, authoritative. Phoebe clung to him, enjoying what he did to her, enjoying the coupling and the fact they were irrevocably joined. Everything was so new that she had no idea what to do to him that would bring him pleasure, but there was plenty of time to learn in the future. All too soon she tipped over the edge once more, and in the seconds before she lost herself to the temporary madness, he stroked inside her again, then his shaft pulsed and jerked. Warmth filled her core, and she gasped.

"Dear God, Phoebe." William ground his hips into hers as he fell into his own bliss. Then he held her so close the steady beat of his heartbeat was in her ears.

"Dear heavens, Frampton, that was wonderful." When she realized she'd inadvertently called him by his title, she still as cold fear twisted down her spine. Had he heard? Was he aware? "I had no idea…"

He snorted. "Does that mean our other couplings were rubbish?" Nothing about his demeanor betrayed the fact that he'd heard her slip.

"No, of course not. Perhaps I'm merely being maudlin." She shoved gently at his shoulder until he lifted himself away and met her gaze. "It was amazing." There was nothing else to do except cling to him, as he held her. With tears in her eyes, Phoebe hugged his neck, and then peppered the column of his throat, his cheek, his temple with kisses. "You are going to be the best father." Why couldn't she stop herself from perpetuating the lies? Sooner or later, she would be found out, and they would both be hurt.

"I look forward to the challenge." When he buried his nose into her hair, she wanted to cry from the trust and intimacy of the gesture. "This was even better the last time we coupled in London."

She froze, for of course, she had never been with him anywhere except in Cranleigh. "Oh?" Did that mean his memories were slowly coming back?

Then he nuzzled the crook of her shoulder. "You're a real brick of a woman, Phoebe. Do you truly think I can make a go of working in the bakery with you over laying bricks? What if we need more income than that?"

How confusing. Was his mind like shifting sand, then? What would happen when more of them surfaced, and he began piecing together his life? She refused to worry about that now, for it would ruin what they had just shared.

"That largely depends on what Aunt Bess will pay in regard to an income. If it's not enough, you could take odd jobs around the village to supplement."

"True." When he rolled onto his back, he tucked her against his side with an arm wrapped around her. "We missed dinner."

For whatever reason, that statement made her giggle. "I made a stew. It's sitting near the fire to stay warm, so no harm was done." There was something satisfying about having a man in her life she could take care of. "Oh, and there's fresh bread and butter."

The rumble of his laughter sent shivers into her chest. "Food for the belly and a wife to make everything comfortable. What more could a man want?"

"What more indeed." Yet as she rested a palm on his naked chest and let her eyes drift closed, knots of worry pulled in Phoebe's belly. Now that they had coupled and she'd lost her innocence, very real consequences could happen. What if she truly fell pregnant and he remembered his life from before? Of course he would want to return to London and his family, which meant he would leave her disgraced and shamed with a babe. How would she support herself as well as an infant? A hot wave of panic rose in her chest. No doubt Aunt Bess would encourage her to give the child to an orphanage or to a couple who couldn't have a baby of their own. It would no doubt prove the best solution, and she certainly didn't want to taint the bakery's business just because she'd decided to lie and live in scandal.

Why did I ever think any of this could work?

"You are tense," he said, and that graveled voice sent delicious tremors through her insides. "What do you worry about? The babe?"

"Out of everything, that is not a concern." Of course it wasn't, since there was no pregnancy. Perhaps it would be easier on all of them if she concocted a story about losing the babe before everything grew too far out of hand. "I suppose I'm worrying over the future." Which was the truth. She was so deeply imbedded in the web of lies she'd already spun, that she had no way of knowing how to extricate herself. Or him. It wasn't fair to him that she'd more or less trapped him into this life not of his own free will. But to be fair, she had no idea who he was or where he belonged.

"We will meet every challenge together. Don't fear things that haven't yet occurred, for they very well might not." When he pressed his lips to the side of her neck, tingles shivered down her spine. "Have I told you how much I adore your body?" he asked into her ear as his stomach rumbled. "I can't have enough of you."

Heated curls of pleasure scudded through her lower belly. "So charming you are."

"Mmm." His wandering fingers slid down her back to squeeze one of her arse cheeks. "There is every possibility I'll bed you again by dawn."

Longing for him throbbed in her core. How could she want him again so soon after what they'd just shared? It was a mystery, for her mother had never had the chance to discuss such things with her before she'd died. "You'll find no argument from me." There was such a thrill in knowing he desired her.

"There is something so... comforting in knowing I have someone like you by my side. It makes me believe I can do anything."

Another round of tears welled in her eyes. It was so unfair that he could be ripped from her life at any moment, and once he realized everything that was between them was a lie? It would devastate her. "You are quite full of gammon, do you know that?" She rose up on an elbow then leaned over to brush her lips along his. Dear heavens, the soft look in his brown eyes would break her if she wasn't careful. "I'm going to find my night clothes then I'll serve your dinner."

His stomach rumbled again, and they shared a laugh. "And in that, I won't argue either." With an indulgent expression on his face, he watched as she slipped from the bed to retrieve her night dress and wrapper from the floor. "Seems a shame you intend to cover that body, but I suppose you can't parade about nude. It might prove dangerous."

Heat went through Phoebe's cheeks. "Do stop, William. You're quite cheeky."

"Can you blame me?"

With a grin, she shook her head. As she dressed, she wondered what his real name was, and what sort of life he'd led in London. After she'd covered herself, she went into the common room where she didn't need to hide her expression from him. If she wanted to discover where he belonged, who would she ask in Cranleigh? And how could she explain, especially after this past week, why she wanted that information? It would ruin her reputation faster than if she truly were pregnant from this coupling, and she couldn't very well put him on the post coach while she remained in Surrey. It would ruin her aunt's business. Only now did she realize everything was connected.

What have I done?

Chapter Nine

October 17, 1817

PHOEBE HUMMED TO herself as she moved freshly cooled jam tarts from a baking sheet to the tray on a wooden shelf behind the counter at the bakery.

Last night with William had exceeded every dream she'd ever had of being a wife. After they'd shared the evening meal as well as a pot of tea—since there was no brandy on hand—they'd settled into a sofa and watched the flames in the hearth fade away. Then once they'd retired to the bedchamber at midnight, she'd been far too aroused and excited to experience intercourse again, so she'd kissed him and dared to explore his body as she'd wished to do before. That had led to a quick and frantic coupling which had been as satisfying as their first one, and if she wasn't careful, she'd find herself in love with the man.

If she wasn't already and those emotions were just hidden beneath the lies.

Aunt Bess glanced at her with speculation in her expression. "You are quite chipper this morning. Is there a particular reason why?"

Heat went through Phoebe's cheeks. "Not really." There was no reason to share with her aunt that she'd been bedded by a man she'd only met seven days ago, the man she was pretending was her husband. "I think I'm finally content with my life." He'd gone out this morning on a couple of errands for her aunt, but she expected him back any moment, and oddly enough, she couldn't wait to work beside him again. How easily she could see them running the bakery in the future, well until they were gray and grandparents.

It's more than I could ever want.

The older woman snorted as she added a few loaves of bread to the shelf. "Your pretend life, you mean?"

"Does it matter at this point?" After last night, she wanted to believe anything was possible… even grasping at a happy ending for herself.

"You are playing with fire, my dear. Don't say I didn't warn you," her aunt said with a sniff. Then she frowned as the door opened at the tin bell above it give its cheerful ring. "Unless I miss my guess, we're both in for it," she warned in a low voice.

"Why?" Phoebe glanced at the man who'd stepped into the bakery.

There was a commanding presence about him as if he alone filled the space of the bakery and demanded their attention. Dressed in the first stare of fashion, his greatcoat had a few capes, his beaver felt top hat sat at a rakish angle over his left eye, his boots had recently been shined, and his buff-colored breeches were impeccably tailored to hug his thighs. A few curls of light brown hair were visible beneath the hat's brim while his hazel eyes were intense as he slid his gaze about the room before resting it on her. Everything about him spoke of upper class, at least of the *ton*.

Phoebe stifled a gasp, for she knew those eyes. In fact, they were the same eyes she'd woken up to for the past week—William's eyes. The knots of worry pulled hard through her belly while icy fingers of apprehension spiraled down her spine. She cleared her throat. "Uh, may I help you?" she asked in a choked voice.

"Yes, quite." The man came forward and paused at the scarred wooden counter. "Lovely bakery, I must say."

Aunt Bess nodded. "Thank you. I've run the place since I was a young woman."

He flicked his gaze between them, finally alighting on Phoebe's face. "I've not visited Surrey for leisure much, and I'm afraid this visit isn't for that either. In fact, I'm here on an urgent mission."

"Oh?" Phoebe's heartbeat accelerated. She couldn't breathe, and with every second that went by, she waited for the second shoe to drop, metaphorically, of course.

"Indeed. I am Lewis Stapleton, the Earl of Lethbridge, and I'm in Cranleigh hoping to find my brother Duncan, or rather Lord Frampton. About a week ago, he came here to fight in a bare-knuckle bout, but then he never returned to London afterward."

Oh, dear God.

Phoebe put a hand to her throat as she stared at the earl. All her lies are on the verge of unraveling, and just as her aunt warned, the stories she'd weaved were crumbling down about her feet. She pressed her lips together. At least she knew who William was now. The son of an earl... the brother of an earl. Essentially, she'd kidnapped, or held an earl's son hostage, in the quest to carve out a bit of happiness for herself. Would she be arrested and tossed into Newgate once they were told of her crimes?

What have I done?

It was Aunt Bess who broke the heavy silence. "I'm sorry to heart that, Your Lordship, but I'm not certain we've seen your brother. Perhaps if you could describe him? He might have wandered away due to a blow to the head."

"Of course, he's..."

Phoebe gripped the counter as the blend of their voices faded into a dull murmur of words she didn't understand. Her head spun and a rush of heat enveloped her form. No longer would she know the contentment she'd finally found; she very nearly fainted as the enormity of what she'd done plowed into her with the force of a blow.

Then the worst thing that could happen… did. The door opened, and as the tin bell tinkled, William, or rather Duncan Stapleton as it were, came into the bakery. The urge to cry out, to beg forgiveness danced on the tip of her tongue, but she couldn't form words, couldn't remember how to talk. He nodded politely at the earl but rested his gaze on her.

"Good morning, Auntie. Good morning, sweeting. I'm ready to don my apron for the day, but first, could I snag one of my favorite jam tarts?"

Another wave of heavy silence filled the interior of the bakery.

Slowly, the earl half turned toward his brother and gawked. "Duncan, what the hell are you doing here? Why haven't you come home?"

With confusion lining his face, her false husband looked at the earl. "I'm sorry, but you must have mistaken me for someone else. I'm William Harris. This is my wife, Phoebe and her aunt who owns the bakery." He offered what he no doubt thought was a disarming smile. "Been a lot of mistaken identities around here lately. Guess I have one of those faces."

"No." The earl shook his head. "None of that is correct. You are Duncan Stapleton, my youngest brother, a son of George Stapleton. You were in prize fight nearly a week ago, have been missing from London ever since you lost the bout." He gestured to his brother's head with a gloved hand. "That wound on your head has no doubt given you amnesia."

"What?" In some surprise, William—Duncan—touched the fading bump at his temple where the bruising was in the process of fading from purple to a greenish yellow color. "No." He shook his head. "I'm a bricklayer and suffered this injury when a brick fell off a wall." With a frown, he bounced his gaze between the three of them. "I assist here in the bakery until I can find better work."

Once more, the dratted tin bell at the door announced the

arrival of yet another person.

This man was younger than the earl by a few years, but there was enough in the way of facial features for her to see that the newcomer was another brother to these two men.

"Duncan? My God, man!" That man embraced William—Duncan—and then loudly slapped him on the back as he stepped away. "We thought we'd lost you, but here you are, as sure as the day is long, standing right here."

The earl cleared his throat. "This is my middle brother Alexander Stapleton—Viscount Wexley." To that man, he said, "These women clearly know something about Duncan's disappearance, but they're calling him William."

Before she could say anything, her fake husband broke the silence. "My good man, you are mistaken. I *am* William Harris, and I live here in this village."

"Enough of this foolishness." The earl cut the air with a hand. "I don't know what nefarious matters are going on here, but is there somewhere all of us can go that is private? Clearly, we need to discuss this issue and what led to Duncan's disappearance."

For the first time, Aunt Bess spoke. "Of course." All the color had leeched from her face. "There are rooms upstairs where my niece and your brother have been living. You can use the common room. I'll put the kettle on and bring up tea."

"Thank you." Then the earl rested his intense gaze on Phoebe. There was no trace of humor or understanding there. "Lead the way, if you please."

She nodded, and with a glance at William—she should refer to him as his real name now, shouldn't she?—and after swallowing a few times to stave off the urge to retch, Phoebe took all the men into the back room and then made her way up the narrow wooden stairs, blinking back the tears that stung her eyes.

He is going to hate me.

And she would lose him.

WHAT THE DEVIL is happening?

Just moments ago, he was told that everything he'd known up until this point had been a lie, that he wasn't who he thought he'd been the past week, that he certainly wasn't married to the woman he'd thought was his wife, that he had a life in London, and that part of said life was being a bare-knuckle boxer of some acclaim.

No wonder he'd felt such an affinity for the sport when that stranger had talked to him in the street in front of the tavern. The man who'd recognized him, and if he'd only pressed the inebriated fellow, he could have discovered the truth sooner than today.

Yet that would have put his whole marriage into jeopardy… except he'd never wed the woman he'd well and truly ruined last night. No wonder he'd had the distinct feeling she'd been an innocent when he'd bedded her, but he thought it was merely a product of his imagination.

Good God, what a coil.

When he glanced at his wife, or rather Miss Phoebe Bidwell as it were, her gaze was cast down to her hands clasped tightly in her lap. His chest tightened, for it meant that everything he'd previously felt her for was suspect. *Shit*, he'd even declared himself to her last night! Like an idiot. And still, when presented with all these facts, there was a part of him that didn't believe what his brothers were telling him.

After clearing his throat, he asked, "How did you find me?"

The man who'd said he was the Earl of Lethbridge flashed a grin. "Oddly, from a youth named Thomas. He lives here in Cranleigh and does odd jobs throughout the village. An errand took him to London for the week, and while he was in Town, he called at my home."

"Why?" None of it made sense.

"Apparently, he remembered your name, for you'd asked him to be your knee man and water boy during the bout because Alexander and I weren't able to come." Guilt and sadness shadowed Lewis' eyes. "He wished to see how you faired after being soundly defeated at the bout." When he shrugged, it only lifted one shoulder. "I should have been there. If I had been, none of this scandal would have occurred."

His other brother, Alexander, nodded as he space the small room. "Having the fellow call added to our worry, especially when we assumed you'd gone straight to your rooms at The Albany, we thought to lick your wounds, so to speak."

Duncan groaned. "And then when I didn't make an appearance at…?"

"The boxing salon that we all own," the earl inserted with a nod.

"When I didn't come 'round there after a few days, you fellows began an inquiry. Correct?"

"Yes." The earl nodded. "I'm afraid we all assumed you'd bedded down with one of the many women you chased." With a frown, he cast a glance to Phoebe, who didn't look up. "It wasn't unusual for you to stay with one for days on end before remembering your responsibilities."

"Ah." Duncan shoved a hand through his hair. No wonder coupling with Phoebe had seemed far too familiar. He'd not bedded her; it had been other women instead. "What the devil should we do now?"

"The only thing we can do." Lewis shoved to his feet. He peered at both of the women in the room then rested his attention on Duncan. "Alex and I are taking you back to London. It's where you belong. It's where your life and your family are."

"That won't be possible. My wife is with child. Or rather, Miss Bidwell is with child, since we are apparently not married." His chest ached as if he'd been hit. The past week had been pleasant and fulfilling. To discover it hadn't been real, that it had only been a farce?

God, I'm going to be ill.

"No, you aren't married." Lewis narrowed his eyes. "If this on-dit finds its way back to London, all hell will break loose, for your last scandal had nearly sent Mama to her bed with smelling salts."

Confusion gripped his mind. It was difficult to discern what was real and what wasn't. "But my babe…"

"William, er, rather Duncan, stop." A blush stained Phoebe's cheeks, and her blue eyes were luminous with the tears welling in them. "I'm not pregnant."

"What?" He put a hand to his chest over his heart where that organ felt as if it were seizing. "It was all part of this false marriage?"

"Yes." Tears fell to her cheeks, and when she brushed at them with her fingers, he grudgingly offered his linen handkerchief. "I'm so sorry. You didn't know who you were… There was nothing I could do…" The delicate tendons in her throat worked with a hard swallow. "You were in a bad state and hurting, so I took care of you. I could have left you wandering on the streets, which would have seen you hurt or perhaps even killed."

"And yet somehow you made the jump from that to us being married?" If his voice rose slightly, he couldn't help it as dual waves of anger and sadness moved through him to form the perfect storm of emotions.

"I know it was wrong, but—"

"It doesn't matter." He held up a hand then sprang up from the low sofa where he and his alleged wife had spent more than a few evenings enjoying… life. "You lied to me, made me think I was your husband, made me think I had a babe on the way, and for what?"

She sniffled. "I was lonely." Then she took refuge in tears once more, hiding her eyes behind the handkerchief.

"As if that makes what you did right." He rubbed the skin above his heart. Damn, her betrayal hurt. Confusion set in, for bits and pieces of his past bubbled up through the muck to collide with what had occurred over the past week. Were the feelings he had for her real, or would they soon vanish since he now knew the truth? And how could one woman manage to manipulate him so soundly? "Did you think to trap me, find a monetary gain in it all?"

That apparently put her dander up, and she glared. "I didn't know who you were, you great nodcock! I was simply doing what I thought was right, and yes, it was selfish of me, but tell me what you would have done in my situation."

Through the haze settling in his brain, he recalled what she'd said about losing everyone in her life she'd ever cared about, and it humbled him. If she'd hadn't given him kindness and caring, what would have become of him?

Lewis cleared his throat. "What is done is done. There is no sense in arguing about it or landing blame. At least you weren't hurt further or taken advantage of by thieves or worse." Then he stood up from his chair. "However, that being said, we *are* taking you back to London where you belong."

The thought of being thrust back into London society and having to do the pretty almost made him physically sick. "But…"

"Also, your pretend wife is coming with us."

Duncan's protest collided with Phoebe's.

"What the devil are you on about?"

"I can't leave Surrey, Your Lordship!"

"Silence, the both of you." His brother held up a hand, and his tone brooked no argument. "I assume you the two of you have lived this past week in sin?" When Duncan nodded, the earl continued. "I'm well within my rights to demand that you both wed truly this time. We can't have any more scandal connected to the name, Duncan. I mean it. There must be an end to your escapades, and perhaps this had to come about to make that happen."

"But—"

His brother shook his head. "No more arguments. You'll have to sleep in the bed you've made for yourself."

"It was Phoebe who made said bed, to be fair. I only believed what I was told."

"He's quite right, Lewis." Alexander chose that moment to chuckle. Amusement danced in his eyes. "Quite literally, Duncan. You can repent at leisure, as the saying goes regardless of whose mess it is, but Lewis will make certain it's done up right and proper this time."

With panic in her expression, Phoebe turned to her aunt. "They can't do that, can they Aunt Bess?"

The older woman shrugged. "It's no longer a question of can they, dear. You made the decision to spin this web that has led to this moment. I rather think you'll need to pay the piper now and clean up your own mess."

She rushed over to her aunt and clung to her hands. "Will you come with me?"

"I have the bakery to run." Sadness battled with protection on her face.

"Papa would never have allowed this to happen."

Her eyes narrowed. "You're right on that. In fact, as soon as he caught wind of what you did, he would have demanded you marry Lord Frampton anyway, so the end result would have been the same." Then her expression softened. "I feel I've spoiled you due to grief over the years, but it's time you learned a few lessons on your own."

"But—"

"Go on, dear. Once you're settled, write to me and let me know how you are. I'll try to visit as soon as I can. All will be well." She looked at Lewis. "Will you allow my niece the time to pack what possessions she has?"

"Of course. I'm not a monster."

Alexander snorted. "That depends on the day." He then glanced at Duncan. "You should pack too."

"Why? I have nothing of value here, and neither does anything belong to me." Belatedly, he met Phoebe's gaze and realized what his words sounded like, especially after everything they'd shared over the past week. Guilt filled his chest. "Damn, I didn't mean it like that."

She stifled a sob. "How could you be so uncaring, regardless that I lied?" Then, as more tears fell to her cheeks, she fled into the bedchamber, with her aunt following quietly on her heels.

"What a damned coil," he muttered, mirroring his earlier thoughts. Could any of it be fixed? Only time would tell.

Chapter Ten

October 20, 1817
Stapleton House
Marylebone, Mayfair
London, England

"WHERE THE HELL do you think you're going?"
Duncan huffed out an annoyed breath as he turned at the foot of the stairs as Lewis was coming down. "What business is it of yours? Don't you have pressing business in the Lords at this time of the afternoon?" It had been three days since his whole world—or the tiny one he thought he'd known—had come crashing down around him. And he'd spent a good portion of that time imbibing brandy.

Damn, he'd missed those spirits while he'd been gone.

"I do, and that is exactly where I'm going, but I wanted to talk with you first."

"Well, I don't wish to talk with you." In fact, now that the swelling at his temple was gone as was the bruising, and being back amidst familiar surroundings, bits and pieces of his memories were slowly coming back. And since they mixed with the new ones he'd made with Phoebe during that week, he had been walking around in a cloud of consternation and confusion.

How the hell did I allow myself to fall for such nonsense?

When Lewis joined him, they walked to the entry hall together. Nearly there, he drew them to a halt and dropped a hand on Duncan's shoulder. "I'm concerned about you."

"So I assumed, since you demanded that I stay here instead of my rooms." Not that he minded. It would have been the first time alone since the bout and the terrifying blow, and within those perimeters, he rather missed his pretend wife. If nothing else, she was a wonderful conversationalist and a refreshing change of pace from the women of the *ton* he usually pursued.

"Beyond that."

Duncan stepped back out of his brother's reach. "How so?"

"Well, you spent a week with a woman to whom you thought you were married, one who'd told you that she carried your child. From what you've told me and Alexander, you were quite happy with the arrangement. In fact, you'd accepted it without much of an argument. Don't you find that odd with the man you truly are?"

Did he? "I don't know, and hell, Lewis, I had no idea *who* I was. What's more, I believed Phoebe."

"I'm aware of that, but surely you must be hurt after everything. You'd cared for her, and she lied. When you expressed feelings for her, did she return them?"

That was something he didn't want to discuss with his brothers. Yes, that betrayal had cut deeply. To say nothing of the odd disappointment that was crushing him. He'd actually enjoyed his life in Surrey, and part of him wished it had been real. But then he'd reminded himself that he wasn't a man who wanted domestication. Or her. Because of that, he'd only seen Phoebe at dinners with the rest of his family, which included his mother and his sisters-in-law.

Because everyone had a mad desire to watch the wreckage of his life, apparently.

"I'm fine." When he tried to move past his brother, Lewis blocked his way. "What?"

"You are marrying the girl tomorrow. How does that make you feel?"

When had his brother started worrying about emotions? "Why the hell do you care?"

"Because you've been through quite the experience, and any man in the same place would come out a bit scarred." Compassion shadowed Lewis' brown eyes. "There is no shame in that, but I need your promise that you will attend your own damned nuptial ceremony. On this I'm quite firm. No more scandal."

I'll be a married man tomorrow morning. Shit.

"I ruined her, so I should pay the price. In this way, everyone gets what they want, except me. How is that any different from any other day?" That wasn't a fair assessment, but he didn't care. In truth, he wanted to yell at the heavens and curse whoever was handy, but he tamped down hard on that urge. There was no point in arguing, for Lewis was stubborn, and he'd just have him married by proxy.

"Good." Lewis nodded. "This might prove for the best, as long as you stay true to her and leave your mistresses behind."

Again, the past and the present collided in his mind. There was no denying that coming home at the end of the day to the same woman had been more pleasing than hopping beds, as had been his wont. Yet being *forced* into a marriage with the same woman felt all too wrong.

"Now, if your lecture is over, I need to borrow your closed carriage." The day was a dismal, overcast one that portended rain at any moment but hadn't started yet.

Lewis frowned. "Why? I need it myself."

"I'll drop you off at the Lords on the way. And if you must know, I'm going over to Mama's house to ask Phoebe to go for a drive with me. There are… things we need to discuss before the morrow." Point of fact, he had to know why she'd done what she did. Everything she'd previously told him had been a lie. What of the feelings he thought she'd had for him? Were they merely an act as well? How would he know if they hadn't been? Did she truly think he wouldn't ever recover his memory? It made no sense.

For long moments, his brother stared at him. Finally, he nodded. "Very well. Your errand is more important, but I expect you home for dinner with your fiancé, and she'd better not be in tears. I've grown weary of that since this whole debacle began."

One corner of Duncan's mouth twitched with the urge to grin. "If she is, can you blame her? The poor girl is staying with Mama. That can't have been a pleasant experience over the past three days."

Lewis chuckled. "You're not wrong. God help her."

Wysteria House
No 12
Hanover Square, Mayfair
London

WHEN HE WAS shown into the drawing room of his mother's house, his nerves felt on edge, for he wasn't of a mind for a lecture or being chided for his behavior.

"Good afternoon, Mama." Duncan crossed the room, took her hand, and then brought it to his lips for a kiss. "I trust you've been keeping yourself well?"

"Don't try to charm me when I'm in a snit with you," she said, but tempered the words with a smile. "While I'm annoyed that you've landed into yet another scandal, I am looking forward to seeing you finally wed."

"I'm glad to have your approval after so long." Though he tamped down on the urge to huff in annoyance, that emotion still bubbled through his chest.

"Whose fault is that?" One of her eyebrows rose. "Why are you here?"

"Why else?" He shrugged. "I wish to take Miss Bidwell… er, rather, Phoebe—" She *had* been his wife in a sense, "For a drive and perhaps a stroll in Hyde Park before the rain starts."

Her face lit. "What a lovely idea." She flashed him another grin. "Truth be told, I have been having a wonderful time coming to know your fiancé more. She's polite and has good looks, but since she's relatively a country bumpkin, she has no decent clothes for being in society."

"No doubt you've taken care of that." It was something he'd not given thought to.

"Of course, and I am thoroughly enjoying the experience since I have only had sons." In fact, his mother did appear glowing. "We've ordered quite a few garments from the local modiste, and I've bought her a lovely gown for the nuptial ceremony tomorrow. At least she'll come to you as a bride should. She's a bit plumper than is perhaps acceptable in society, but she's a pretty young woman all the same."

As if a woman's weight or size determined whether she was attractive. Another wave of annoyance rose in his chest, yet he recalled how marvelous Phoebe's form had felt against his and how much he'd adored acquainting himself with her curves. "If you could fetch her for me? I'd like to make the best use of the time before the rain sets in. You know how damp the autumn is."

"Of course." His dowager mother rose to her feet and shook out her ivory and purple striped skirting. "It's good you wish to spend time with her; you've both been quite hurt from what happened in Surrey."

He didn't answer as she left the room, for he didn't trust himself to voice those thoughts, but ultimately, he couldn't continue ignoring the woman who would become his wife tomorrow morning.

The rustle of fabric heralded the arrival of the ladies, and as he turned toward them, his heart oddly skipped a beat as he caught his first glance at her in the daylight since they were forced back to London by his brothers.

Clad in a day dress of a deep maroon color with long sleeves and a plain bodice, she was almost the embodiment of autumn. His mother had done a wonderful job at outfitting Phoebe, for her blonde hair had been upswept and held into place with a pair of tortoiseshell combs. A necklace of small pearls encircled her neck that provided a touch of elegance without being vulgar. A pair of matching pearl earbobs hung at her lobes.

"Good afternoon, Lord Frampton," she managed in a trembling whisper, with a hint of a blush in her round cheeks. "Lady Lethbridge informed me that you wish to take me driving."

What the hell? His mother demanded she call her by the title? With a frown, he glanced at his parent, but she stared back with expectation. "I do, and we are to be married tomorrow. Please refer to me as Duncan."

She nodded, but an air of sadness clung to her. "Thank you." When she finally raised her gaze to his, his world tilted a bit, for those damned blue eyes glimmered like gemstones.

"I thought it the best venue to talk." How well he remembered her eyes, remembered her from before the lies started as the young woman who'd stood on the outskirts at the bout when they'd locked gazes, and she'd turned his world on its ear. "And I thought you might enjoy an outing since you've been stuck inside for a few days."

When she frowned, he was struck that her bottom lip was slightly fuller than the top. "Why?"

"Why not?" Duncan shrugged, and hated that his mother watched them like a hawk. "If I'm to marry you tomorrow, I damn well need to know who you really are."

"For shame, Duncan. Where are your manners?" his mother chided.

"I apologize." He nodded. "Phoebe, would you like to accompany me on a drive? Perhaps a walk in Hyde Park if the weather holds?"

"Yes, thank you."

His mother patted her arm. "I sent your pelisse to the butler. He'll help you into it in the entryway."

And then he escorted his fiancé out of the drawing room. There was no going back now.

Hyde Park
Mayfair

UNFORTUNATELY, SHE WAS quiet on the drive to Hyde Park. Though it hadn't started raining, the air had the feel of that happening quite soon. To be fair, Duncan hadn't a clue how to begin the conversation. How did one manage a polite talk with a woman who'd basically kidnapped him and pretended that he was her husband, a woman who'd manipulated his emotions? They more or less vanished into their own thoughts until arriving at the park.

After he assisted her out of the carriage, he instructed the driver to wait for them, that they shouldn't be out for more than an hour, then he tucked Phoebe's hand into the crook of his arm and began their walk.

In silence.

No sooner than they reached a spot deep in the park than a steady, cold rain began.

"Shit." Duncan grabbed hold of her hand. "There!" He pointed to a small stone structure that had a crumbling roof. The whole thing resembled an old Roman temple, no doubt a folly for decoration. Hadn't Alex told him about this spot in the park and how he'd made use of it with his wife when he'd been courting her? "It's the only shelter in the immediate area, and quite frankly, I don't fancy being cold and wet just now."

"Neither do I," Phoebe said as she hitched up her skirts and ran beside him until they reached the folly. Then she laughed, but there was only a trace of mirth in the sound. "That about sums up our lives for the past week or so, doesn't it?"

"It does." The chill in the air was exacerbated by the rain. "Please, sit." He gestured at a stone bench. "We might be here a while." Once she did, he frowned at her. There was no reason to delay this conversation. "Why did you do it, Phoebe?" Despite wishing to remain nonchalant about it, emotion graveled his voice.

"Do what?"

He huffed. "You know what."

"I have no excuse." She shrugged as she focused her gaze outside their makeshift shelter as she clasped her gloved hands in her lap. "Other than what I've already told you; I was lonely."

"So you decided to make up a whole life and reel me into it?" Merely saying she was lonely wasn't enough to justify the emotional gambit she'd put him through. "What the hell?"

She flinched as if he'd hit her, and he told himself to moderate his tone when next he spoke. "You have no idea how difficult it is to be one of the sole survivors of your family." Not once did she look at him. "Because you still have your mother and your brothers, you haven't experienced the sort of loneliness or emptiness that I constantly struggle with, that grief that attacks with no warning." A long-suffering sigh escaped her. "Add to that the loss of two fiancés, and there aren't many things to look forward to."

The words humbled him and took the edge off his annoyance. "I'm sorry for the deaths you have had in your circle, but—"

"No." Phoebe shook her head. She raised her gaze and found his. Sadness and guilt warred for dominance in those depths. "Without my Aunt Bess, I don't know what would have become of me, for I long ago grew tired of grieving, and I am sick of having people leave me." Then she narrowed her eyes while a trace of determination went through her expression. He admired her for that. "When you came along, I saw that as an opportunity to grasp at a bit of happiness for myself after all the struggles. I'd hoped your memories might stay missing so that we could enjoy a life together."

"Well, some of them are coming back the more I heal. Having familiar surroundings and people about is helping."

"I see." She nodded. "I'm glad for you, then. Clearly, this is the world in which you belong and where you thrive."

There was so much dejection in the statement that his chest tightened. *God, I've been a cad.* To be fair, he'd been taken advantage of, and had gone along with the story because he hadn't known better. Did everyone assume he was a pushover and could be trifled with? "Answer me another question?" When she nodded, he continued. "Why did you say you were pregnant?"

"I was afraid you might leave anyway after my aunt questioned you. I needed a way to make you stay, for I was just beginning to acclimate to having you in my life, to... care for you."

And now all of that was gone, smashed due to her lies. Still, his heart ached. "Oddly, I wanted that child." It was a difficult admission for him because he wasn't a family man.

"Again, I apologize. I didn't give thought to the fact my lies would hurt so many people." Her eyes welled with tears. "I couldn't stop once I started, yet I also couldn't just turn you out into the night and wish you well."

"While I understand that, you could have at least told the truth, that I was a stranger who'd lost his memories."

"Would you have stayed?"

For the space of a few heartbeats, he remained silent. "I don't know." It seemed he wasn't certain of anything these days. With a shrug, he sighed and steeled himself against her tears. Were they even genuine? "Regardless, I'm sorry for your losses."

Her shrug only lifted one shoulder. "It is life."

Not wanting to be sucked into another emotional quagmire, he temporarily glanced away from her. "Now you'll have the husband you always wanted." Unfortunately, there was much bitterness in his tone that he couldn't tame.

"Quite frankly, I don't want that." When she stood, Phoebe went to the edge of the folly with her back to him. "I lost the man you were before, the man I was going to build a life with; because of what I've done, things between us will never be the same, regardless that we're being forced to wed." When she turned to face him, the tears in her eyes fell to her cheeks and she sniffled. "I didn't want any of this to happen. It's pathetic, I know, and sounds horrid when said aloud. I just wanted someone by my side, someone who needed me for me."

Shit, shit, shit.

Pain radiated around Duncan's heart, but he ignored it the best he could. Neither of them were the same people they'd been last week. Everything had changed, and now he couldn't trust her. "I don't want to be domesticated, never have. I want to return to my old life."

"Of being nothing?" One of her blonde eyebrows rose in question, and the backbone she showed impressed him, for it appeared she would rally. To fight, and that he understood. "Of always waiting to see if the debt collectors will catch you up? Or perhaps it's to return to chasing skirts and finding your next mistress?"

"What the devil are you on about?" The sound of the heavy rain dulled the rising tones of their voices.

"Your mother told me the sort of man you truly are, told me about all the scandals, the women, the gambling, the pockets always to let, the way you skirt responsibility. I couldn't believe it at first, for the man I'd known in Surrey was exactly the oppo- site." She took a few steps toward him over the small expanse of stone floor. "And now I see that it was true all along, and I was the fool for thinking you could be anything else."

How the devil she'd managed to turn the blame of the con- versation onto him he would never know, but he didn't like it. Hot ire rose in his chest. "You let me bed you, thinking we'd already done that multiple times during a false marriage." When he shoved a hand through his hair, he knocked his top hat off. It fell to the stone floor with a dull thud. "And you an innocent the whole time! Hell, how did you know I would have consented to any of that?"

"You were *quite* interested." Color stained her cheeks. "Things happened far too quickly. I was swept away, but I don't regret any of that. At least I won't die an old maid."

There were no signs of malicious intent in her expression, and those damned tears just kept falling, dragging him down into an emotional pit again. For a long time, Duncan stared at her, and to be honest, he struggled with how he felt about the whole thing. It was one thing for him to seduce a woman and then leave her the next day, but it was quite another to have the same scenario done to him. Yet what she'd done was worse. She'd lied to him, told him they'd been married, that they were expecting a baby, all so she could manipulate him into staying with her due to loneliness. An empty feeling grew within his chest. Yet again, he'd only been wanted for something he could give to someone.

"Well, bully for you. At least you got what you wanted from me, huh?" It would seem he would forever be testy around everyone in his life.

"That's not all of it. What you and I had for a week…" Her swallow was audible. "I'll never forget, for it was the best time in my life."

"Yet we will truly be wed tomorrow." Why was this so confusing? And more to the point, why the devil did he care?

"It won't be the same, and you'll go into it with no intentions of being a faithful husband." There was so much desperation in her voice that the urge to cast up his accounts grew strong.

"Perhaps, but you don't have the right to make that—or any—decisions for me." Yes, he was angry—livid, in fact—for what she'd done to him, and yes, he felt empathy for her reasoning, but none of that meant he should be forced into something he didn't want. Did he? While enjoying the fake marriage, there had been a decided feeling of belonging, as if he'd finally found his place in the world. All that had been yanked away, and it left him at sixes and sevens.

Was it because he was grieving what had happened to him, or was he still longing for something he obviously didn't have?

"I understand that. I do, but once again, I will be alone, except this time I'll be trapped in a world where I don't belong."

Well, damn.

His heart squeezed, for that butted up against what he'd just thought. Emotions came at him from all sides, and he didn't wish to relive any of them, for he'd been a fool in Surrey because he'd thought himself in love with her. *Well, that won't happen again.* Tamping down tight on those feelings, he looked at her again as she stood there with tears rolling down her cheeks, and as it turned out, he wasn't as strong as he thought. How was it that he could fight men in a boxing ring, yet the sight of a woman's tears left him wilting?

"Come here." Duncan reeled her into his arms, and though she fought against him, eventually, she went pliant with a soft sob and melted into his hold.

"I wish this hadn't happened? It's hurt us both, just like my aunt warned me it would. Frankly, this is worse than feeling lonely," she said, and her words were muffled by his cravat.

"Agreed, but as you said, it is life. We must endure it, mistakes, triumphs, all of it. Sometimes our reckoning comes, and there is naught we can do except meet it." Despite his confusion, he put a curled finger beneath her chin, lifted her head, and then gently fitted his lips to hers in a gentle kiss designed to offer comfort. And the embrace was as contenting and exciting as he remembered, damn it all to hell. There was history between them, more than what he usually had with a mistress, and there was something... comforting in that.

But he didn't want a wife, especially a woman who'd already fed him a string of untruths.

Did he?

Chapter Eleven

October 21, 1817
Stapleton House
Marylebone, Mayfair
London, England

"I DON'T THINK I can do this," Phoebe admitted to Aunt Bess as they stood outside the drawing room at the Earl of Lethbridge's townhouse. "And this gown, though lovely, is far too fancy and luxurious for someone like me."

Her aunt tsked her tongue. "Hush, dear. If the dowager countess wished to spend her coin on this gown, and everything else she's already given you, why contest it? You are marrying into a family of the *beau monde*. You will need to square with that and whatever comes with it." She lowered her voice. "But it is quite a beautiful gown."

"I'm not worthy of this," Phoebe argued in a barely audible whisper as she slid her hands down the front of the expensive gown. "Lady Lethbridge said the modiste had copied the design from a drawing she'd seen in *Ackermann's Repository*. She told me it's a gown for a young lady of high distinction and made of striped French gauze over cream satin with a deep flounce of Brussels lace." She shook her head and couldn't stop touching the frothy confection that reminded her of something Aunt Bess would make in the bakery. "The dowager said I could reuse the gown as a ball gown, for surely once Duncan was wed, invitations would come his way."

"Well, she's not wrong, on either count. Reusing a gown saves coin. I especially like the line of roses and leaves that rest right above the flounce."

Phoebe glanced down. "They are made of pink and green satin ribbon. It must have taken the seamstresses hours." Then she sighed. "However, the dowager managed not to pay full price."

"Oh, why?"

"The young lady's mother, who ordered this gown, changed her mind, so the modiste didn't receive payment. Buying it with only a few alterations because we were nearly the same size meant savings for the dowager and coin for the modiste."

"Stop worrying, and stop downplaying this day." Aunt Bess dropped her hands on Phoebe's shoulders. She held her gaze. "You are a beautiful bride. Though you lied to gain exactly this, I hope this time 'round you'll learn from your previous mistakes. What you found with Duncan before, you'll find again. I can almost guarantee it."

"I don't know." She blinked away the tears that stung her eyes. Those words he'd whispered to her the night they'd coupled rang in her ears. Would he ever mean them again? "He is quite miffed with me, and I rather doubt I'm interesting enough to hold his attention. Apparently, Lord Frampton is very happy being a gentleman about Town." She touched a gloved finger to the lace lining the short, puffed sleeves of the gown. "I don't fit into his world."

"Don't talk rubbish. You are resourceful, and people will adore you." Aunt Bess winked. "Never discount the power of love, dear."

Worry pulled the knots in her belly. "It's not only that. The earl told us this morning that he put down a payment on a modest townhouse in Bedford Square as a wedding gift. Instead of Duncan paying the rents on his rooms, he can take that coin and make payments on the townhouse until he's able to buy it outright." She shook her head as her chest tightened. "Why is the Stapleton family being so generous to me? I'm no one."

"Stop, my girl." Authority rang in Aunt Bess' voice. "Out of anyone in this world, you deserve fine things and happiness. Let them help you and pamper you in the ways your parents or even I could never do." She patted Phoebe's cheek. "You are going to sail through this transition just like you always have." She glanced into the drawing room. "It seems that the vicar and your husband-to-be are anxious to begin the ceremony. Are you?"

Phoebe shrugged. "No, but that won't stop it."

Aunt Bess tugged her into the doorway. "Buck up, dear. This is your path now. It would behoove you to carve out some happiness there, for you would never have had this opportunity before he came along." Her voice broke. "Your parents would be proud of you."

"I wish they were here today."

"In spirit, dear. In spirit."

Straightening her spine, Phoebe moved into the drawing room with Aunt Bess at her side. There were far too many guests assembled in the space. She knew the members of Duncan's family, and the rest must be friends of the dowager and associates of the earl. In total, there were probably twelve people, all there to whisper and gossip about what she'd done that had led them here today.

Well, they can all bugger off. I'm not happy about this either.

Then her gaze met that of Duncan's, and the intensity therein sent a host of flutters into her lower belly, and like a ninny, she forgot how to breathe when presented with him clad in his dark suit and tailcoat. She couldn't read many of the emotions in those brown depths, but there *was* admiration in his expression.

To her aunt, she whispered, "It's unfortunate that he is so handsome this morning." The waistcoat of sapphire blue silk had been embroidered with silver stars and called her attention to his flat abdomen that she well remembered from their time within the sheets.

"Why is that?"

"It makes today all the more difficult."

Aunt Bess chuckled. "Contretemps and hurt feelings will be smoothed over with understanding and compromise." She patted Phoebe's hand. "Have faith in yourself and him." Then they arrived at the spot where Duncan and an older man stood in front of the fireplace where a cheerful fire danced behind an ornamental metal frame that looked like a peacock with full tail. She put Phoebe's hand on his sleeve. "Best wishes to you both." Then she left to find a seat within the sea of guests.

Before she could say anything to Duncan, the tall, slender, older man offered a faint grin. He had a full head of snow-white hair and deep lines in his kind face.

"I am Mr. Cochran, and I will be officiating your nuptial ceremony. My clerk, Mr. Simpson is waiting at the back of the room with the register you'll need to sign afterward."

Duncan nodded. "If you don't mind, let us move forward with this."

"Ah, an eager bridegroom. It's good to see," Mr. Cochran said, clearly immune to the tension fairly crackling between them. He retrieved a well-worn leather copy of *The Book of Common Prayer* from the mantle. "If everyone could settle, the nuptial couple is ready to begin."

Though she would have liked to speak privately with her fiancé before the ceremony, there was no time. Nerves fluttered in Phoebe's stomach but calmed somewhat when Duncan took her hand and threaded it through his crooked elbow.

"Dearly beloved, we are gathered together here in the sight of God, and in the face of these witnesses, to join together this Man and this Woman in holy Matrimony; which is an honorable estate, instituted of God in the time of man's innocency, signifying unto us the mystical union that is betwixt Christ and his Church…"

Dear heavens, this is truly happening.

After losing her previous two fiancés, she had lost hope in ever thinking she would eventually find herself wed. Now she stood next to the son of an earl, preparing to speak vows to him, but not with love present for the union. Phoebe clung to his arm and the scent of him teased her nose with a blend of sage, citrus, and sandalwood. It was quite lovely and something he didn't have during his stint as her pretend husband. Oddly, his strength calmed her nerves, for regardless of why they'd arrived here, she knew he was capable of being a kind and compassionate man.

Would he allow that person to shine through after today?

It wasn't until he discreetly and softly cleared his throat that she ceased her wool-gathering and attended to what Mr. Cochran said as he addressed Duncan.

"Wilt thou have this Woman to thy wedded Wife, to live together after God's ordinance in the holy estate of Matrimony? Wilt thou love her, comfort her, honor, and keep her in sickness and in health; and, forsaking all others, keep thee only unto her, so long as ye both shall live?"

Phoebe trembled; her breath held in anticipation. Did he truly understand the severity of those words? Would he stay faithful to her and give up his wicked ways?

After uttering a cough, Duncan answered, "I will." Though it sounded as if he said it through gritted tea.

Phoebe's jitters increased, as the minister addressed her.

"Wilt thou have this Man to thy wedded Husband, to live together after God's ordinance in the holy estate of Matrimony? Wilt thou obey him, and serve him, love, honor, and keep him in sickness and in health; and, forsaking all others, keep thee only unto him, so long as ye both shall live?"

Hadn't she already shown him that she would after caring for him? Surely that must excuse the lie. She glanced over her shoulder to locate her aunt, who gave her an encouraging nod. Then, she nodded as her hand trembled upon Duncan's arm. "I will." Her answer came out breathless and in a whisper, for tears crowded in her throat.

Will our union fail before it ever starts?

He was instructed to take her right hand in his right hand, and hers shook so badly that he gently squeezed her fingers. He went so far as to put his lips to her ear and whisper, "Despite our current… difficulties, this is not a prison sentence."

"Do you think that for yourself as well?" she inquired back in a whisper of her own.

With his eyes clear and honesty in his expression, he gave a curt nod. "Yes."

"Oh." Phoebe smiled lest he think she looked upon the ceremony with dread. Which she did, to a point, but only because her sins had landed them here to begin with.

Will he ever love me again? Is it possible that I'll fall for the man he is now?

The vicar cleared his throat and continued. "Lord Frampton, repeat after me…" He intoned words that Phoebe scarcely heard until Duncan said them to her.

"I, Duncan Matthew Stapleton, Lord Frampton, take thee Miss Phoebe Elizabeth Bidwell to my wedded Wife, to have and to hold from this day forward, for better for worse, for richer or poorer, in sickness and in health, to love and to cherish," he stumbled over those words, but quickly recovered, "'till death us do part, according to God's holy ordinance; and thereto I plight thee my troth." When his gaze collided with hers, she gasped at the intensity there.

What was he thinking?

They were directed to release hands, and Phoebe was told to then hold Duncan's right hand with her right hand. "Ahem." The vicar addressed her. "Miss Bidwell, repeat after me." He gave her the words, and she prayed she would say them all in the proper order and not make a fool out of herself due to nerves.

"I, Miss Phoebe Elizabeth Bidwell, take thee Duncan Matthew Stapleton, Lord Frampton to my wedded Husband." She paused to swallow. "To have and to hold from this day forward, for better for worse, for richer or poorer, in sickness and in health, to love, cherish, and to obey, 'till death us do part, according to God's holy ordinance." She lowered her voice to a whisper. "And thereto I give thee my troth." How slightly terrifying such a thing was.

Please let me show him—and myself—this isn't a mistake.

They were instructed to again release their hands. Duncan gave a ring to the vicar, who then laid it upon his open *Book of Common Prayer* and then her soon-to-be husband offered a small leather purse of what she assumed was a form of payment for services rendered. She needed to remember to ask Duncan about it later. Then Mr. Cochran returned the ring to Duncan, and she quickly tugged the glove from her left hand. He slipped it onto the fourth finger of that hand, and she couldn't help but admire the silver band set with small, oval-shaped sapphires and aquamarine gemstones that winked in the candlelight, for the morning was, of course, overcast.

Mr. Cochran directed him to repeat another set of words while she quickly tugged on her glove.

"With this Ring I thee wed, with my Body I thee worship, and with all my worldly Goods I thee endow. In the Name of the Father, and of the Son, and of the Holy Ghost. Amen."

Oh, heavens, we are truly wed.

"I will invite everyone in attendance to pray for the new nuptial couple," Mr. Cochran offered with a grin.

In much awkwardness, Phoebe kneeled when Duncan did, still clutching his hand while her thoughts spun. As the words of a prayer droned on, she closed her eyes and sent up a simpler prayer of her own, asking for strength to survive what would surely be a difficult adjustment to a brand-new life, one she had no knowledge about.

I don't know if I'm capable of any of this.

He leaned over, and with his lips at the shell of her ear, he whispered, "I will teach you everything you need to know; despite why we have had to wed, I won't let you fall. I know what it's like feeling as if you'll disappoint everyone around you."

A tremor set up around her heart, and she nodded. Perhaps this wouldn't be as big a mistake as she assumed.

When she and Duncan stood, Mr. Cochran intoned, "I now pronounce thee husband and wife."

And then it was over. Polite clapping went through the assembled guests.

No longer was she the pleasantly plump country bumpkin, Phoebe Bidwell who'd suffered more grief in a lifetime than anyone should. And, good heavens, she would miss her aunt and the bakery! Now, she was Lady Frampton, the wife of a prize fighter and a co-owner of a boxing salon.

The vicar smiled. "If you could just sign the register?" Then he addressed the witnesses. "I am told the wedding breakfast is ready to be served across the hall in the dining room, if you would like to join the dowager countess there."

When Duncan applied pressure to Phoebe's upper arm, she accompanied him to the small table near the windows where the clerk sat where they both signed the registry, which made the union official.

Only then did she overhear a few snatches of whispers as some of the guests she didn't know drifted from the room.

"...wed in haste, repent in leisure. Does anyone know who she is? He'll throw her over for a mistress soon..."

"...why did he choose her when he could have married someone from the *ton*..."

"...a man as handsome as him is certainly wasted on her..."

With every word, Phoebe died a little more inside. Instead of the joyous—somewhat—occasion, the day brought instead a murky future. The desire to cry silly tears for fear she'd made a mistake climbed her chest. Why had Duncan chosen to marry her when she was vastly unsuited for the position? Surely, the gossips would shred whatever remained of her reputation.

And he would come to resent her.

The Countess of Lethbridge came to her rescue. She grabbed one of Phoebe's hands and squeezed in support. "Don't listen to those women. Stiff upper lip, Phoebe, and remember. The best revenge is to show naysayers that you are, indeed, succeeding and thriving." She patted Phoebe's hand. "I know you're made of sterner stuff than they think. Duncan wouldn't have picked you otherwise."

"I shall try my best, but he *didn't* choose me. He was forced to do this," Phoebe whispered. She stumbled over to a window. After unlocking the latch, she gently pushed open the glass and breathed in lungsful of the crisp autumn air in an effort to stem the welling tears.

"The fight is only just starting," the countess whispered as she patted Phoebe's shoulder. "Stapleton men don't go down easily, and you'll need to fight—sometimes fiercely—for what you want out of life. Including them."

She nodded. "Thank you." That made sense even if she didn't understand the boxing part of her new husband's life.

Duncan joined them and thanked the countess for coming. As she went off to find the earl, he slipped an arm about her waist. "The first rule of understanding life in the *beau monde* is acknowledging that there are vipers in our midst. Don't let them bite you, and don't mind their barbs."

"Duncan is quite correct." This from his middle brother, Viscount Wexley, who beamed at her with amusement sparkling in his eyes. "We've all landed in the mire before, and Duncan many more times than the rest of us. The trick is to ignore them."

"It is quite difficult, though. I'm afraid I'll embarrass myself and all of you, when you've been nothing but lovely toward me."

Her new husband snorted. "Except me." But he kept his hand at the small of her back, and she appreciated the warmth of the connection.

Again, she breathed in the fresh outside air as the remainder of the guests filtered from the room. "You have good reason."

Viscount Wexley shook his head. "Nonsense. You're a Stapleton now, and have a family behind you to fight for you. It makes all the difference." Coming close, he bussed her cheek. "Congratulations, Lady Frampton. I look forward to knowing you better." With a wink at Duncan, he said, "I should find my wife. Otherwise, she'll have much to say about my tardiness."

Then she was alone with her husband.

At the door to the room, Mr. Cochran and his clerk lingered to talk with a couple of guests in low tones, but the full of her attention was on Duncan.

"I meant what I said earlier. I'll school you on the peers and their wives in the *ton*, who to befriend and who to avoid, which causes and charities you might wish to dip a toe into." A muscle ticced in his cheek. "It's the least I can do now that you've ultimately gotten what you wanted after having me compromise you in Cranleigh."

"I apologized for that. How many times must I continue doing so?" Would he hold that over her head for the length of their union? What a bitter existence, if so.

"I realize that, but that doesn't mean I'm not still angry."

Fair enough. "I'm angry too." She forced down a hard swallow. "I never wanted a husband who doesn't want me." If she were ever going to stand toe-to-toe with him and rest on level ground so to speak with him, she'd need to fight. Not that she had any idea how to do that either. "If you hadn't continually caused your family embarrassment with multiple scandals each year, perhaps we wouldn't be here, for your family was merely looking for an excuse for you to be married. I was a convenient scapegoat."

That was the truth. It wasn't so much her indiscretion and lies, but his family's wish to tamp down on having Duncan run amok through London.

His eyes flashed anger. "So then all of you have neatly managed to trap me. Bravo, Lady Frampton. Well played."

"Enough." Phoebe blew out a breath. "If you feel trapped, so do I." She went as far as to stamp a slipper-clad foot in her aggravation. "I don't want to tame you, Will... er Duncan. I like you as you are, or were, for I don't know the you of London."

Lightly, she bit her bottom lip, and his gaze dropped to her mouth. Tears welled in her eyes. "Frankly, I'm terrified of this new life. I wasn't bred for it; I'm a country girl, from a simple life. I know nothing about the *beau monde*, and because of that, I'll embarrass you. And that is never what I wanted from what is between us."

"Calm yourself, Phoebe." He pressed his handkerchief into her hand. "I have never learned how to guard my words. They just flow out of my mouth as soon as I think of them, regardless of if they are hurtful."

"You have every right to speak your mind." She dabbed at the corners of her eyes with the pocket square. "So do I."

"Perhaps, but I can see how we have been tossed into the ring, so to speak, and have been told to battle it out despite what we both might have wanted… before."

The concession was unexpected, but it gave her a modicum of comfort. She shook her head. "This is my life now—ours I suppose—and perhaps my penance for tricking you. However, if you betray our wedding vows, I deserve that for what I did, and there is nothing I can do that will make things right again." She sniffled and wiped her nose.

"Infidelity is never anything a wife or husband should suffer through." When he cupped her cheek, she nearly melted into him from the unexpected touch. His eyes softened as he looked at her. "If you do penance, then so must I, for I was far more scandalous by myself than with you."

A tear fell to her cheek. "Please say you forgive me. I never wished to hurt you, and I hope…" She swallowed. "Well, I hope we can find our way to friendship again."

His expression crumpled, and for one terrible moment, she assumed he might cry, but he mastered his emotions. "Of course I forgive you. How can I hold you in judgment when I'm as guilty?" But there were shadows in his eyes, and hurt. He wiped away the tear with the pad of his gloved thumb. "We need to move past what happened in Surrey."

"How? It's one reason we are here." Would she ever be able to gain his trust again?

"I don't know, but like we did then, we will muddle through."

She nodded. "Thank you."

A wave of silence brewed between them.

Finally, Duncan blew out a breath and gave himself a shake. Then, he bestowed a grin on her. "Well, there are worse people to spend the time with, hmm? You and I got on well enough before." When he shrugged, her attention was taken up with the breadth of his shoulders. "It's rather lovely to have a partner in scandal this time 'round, and your indiscretion has taken the focus off me for a change." His grin widened while amusement twinkled in his eyes. Clearly, he was trying to joke and break the tension.

It cheered her, but only just. Then she couldn't help it, and a snort of laughter escaped her tight throat. Phoebe gave his chest a playful slap. "Don't be more of an idiot than you can help… Duncan."

"Ha." He winked, and flutters went through her lower belly. "Thank you for the reminder. Let us go into breakfast. I'm famished."

"Aren't you always?"

Her husband didn't answer. Instead, he drew her hand through his crooked shoulder and led her from the room.

How am I going to survive this frightening new life?

Chapter Twelve

October 23, 1817
No 10
Bedford Square, Mayfair

I T HAD BEEN two days since he'd legally wed Phoebe and they'd moved into the modest townhouse in Bedford Square. Thank God most of the rooms were already furnished; Lewis must have done some fast talking in order to land a contract like that. Otherwise, he and his new bride would be sleeping and doing everything else on the floor.

And since none of the guest room beds had tick mattresses, for the past two nights, he and Phoebe had shared the main bed. Had that been part of Lewis' plan when he'd rented the townhouse, to force him and his new wife together? Damn his eyes. But the staff he'd hired seemed well-organized and worked well as a staff.

Another item of domestication was the fact that Phoebe's aunt had gifted them with new linens to dress their marriage bed. The sumptuous silk bed clothes featured navy and cream colors, and one of his sisters-in-law had outfitted the room with heavy navy drapes at the windows and around the bed. Clearly, they'd worked together, but it made for a comfortable nest, and having Phoebe beside him was comforting.

That had proved a test of his control, for as much as he wanted to consummate their real marriage, he was unable to sort through his feelings for her. Yes, he'd been courtesans or a mistress for much less, but it was different with Phoebe. Each morning he woke and saw her round cheeks, the blonde mess of her hair on the pillows, and the eager hopefulness in her blue eyes, he wanted to throw himself onto his knees beside the bed and beg her forgiveness merely so he could have her naked and writhing beneath him.

Yet that wouldn't have been fair to either of them.

Instead, they'd interacted with each other as if they were friends attempting to play house.

Today, he rose around noon, and eventually he found her in the room that he'd claimed for his study. As of yet, the desk was empty, as were the wooden shelves and the sideboard, but the leather chair behind the desk still had life in it, and it only squeaked when he leaned to the left.

"Phoebe, why are you in here?"

She turned toward him with a slight smile. "Since we don't have a library in our house, I'm considering using your study in that regard. We can share the shelf space between us."

"Sure." He leaned a shoulder against the door frame. "Except I'm not one for reading or collecting books. I'm more a newspaper man or I have conversations with men at my club."

"Oh." There was such a crestfallen expression on her face that he immediately wanted to erase it. "There is so much I don't know about you and your life now."

Being uprooted from the country and dumped into the faster pace of London must be difficult for her. "However, I would be delighted to share the room with you. While I work on the account ledgers for the household or my investments, you can read to your heart's content." In fact, as he glanced about the room with its heavy furniture of richly stained walnut wood and dark leather upholstery, he could easily envision the two of them passing long winter's nights here in front of the fireplace. "Feel free to visit a few booksellers this week and select volumes that you think we'll find interesting or engaging."

"Truly?" Delight danced in her eyes.

"Of course." He nodded and pushed off the door frame. "And while you're out, think about how you might wish to decorate our home."

Dear God, was there any word more comforting than *home*? And he only just realized that he'd not had such a feeling since he was a youth.

"I would like that. Lydia said she would take me 'round the shops in a few days." She frowned the longer she rested her gaze on him. "What are you plans for the day?"

"I'm scheduled at the boxing salon for general public lessons and to help with open floor bouts." He shrugged and closed the distance between them. "If my brothers are there, I need to speak with them about a few things, and afterward, I must call on my solicitor to have paperwork drawn up now that I have a wife to care for." Those words echoed the ones he'd said to her nearly two weeks ago when he'd vowed to look after her.

And the babe she'd lied about. Was she even now carrying his child from that one, blissful night when they'd coupled? Did he want to be a father?

"Will I see you at dinner or do you go to your club? Isn't that what men of the *ton* do?"

Ordinarily, but he was a newly married man. If he showed up at his club, he'd be a laughingstock. "No, I'll be here. Perhaps we should plan a short wedding trip."

Surprise lined her expression. "Do we have the money for that?"

"No, but I would imagine if I broached the subject around my mother, she might be inclined to help us with that." He shrugged. "I'm the baby of the family and have no shame, remember?" Then, with a wink, he tugged her close. "Will you be all right rattling around here on your own?"

"I think so. Later, your mother is coming by to take me to a tea café and then around to call on a few of her friends as a slow introduction into society." Apprehension jumped into her eyes. "I hope I'm good enough for those women."

"If my mother didn't think you were, she wouldn't have invited you, for she has a vast network of friends and acquaintances. Hell, you'll probably come back with a handful of invitations to various events."

God help us all. Was there any point in attending functions if he couldn't flirt with the women there?

"Only time will tell." But her chin trembled. "I miss Aunt Bess. She'd be there to help me through."

He held her close, and encouraged her head to rest on his chest. "Why don't you write to her before you go out with Mama? We shall try to get out to Cranleigh once a month, weather permitting. Would you like that?"

"Yes." The word was muffled by his jacket.

The scent of lavender and lemon teased his nose, and it was quite different than the smell of vanilla and baked goods he'd known of her previously. Someone must have given her a bottle, but it was no less alluring. "I should go," he said as he pulled slightly away, but suddenly, he didn't want to leave her or their new home, and because he couldn't help it, Duncan dipped his head and claimed her lips.

Bloody hell, but the tiny moan turned sigh she uttered as she looped her arms about his shoulders nearly broke him, for every inch of him remembered what she had felt like in his bed, and how satiny her skin was against his fingers and lips, and how damned tight her passage had been that first time he'd claimed her. After settling her more securely in his embrace, he kissed her with more intensity, moving his mouth over hers then daring to seek out her tongue with his.

Since Phoebe had always been a quick study, it took next to no time for her to match his overtures, and soon he was guided by heated desire and the insistent pulse of his member. If he didn't stop, he'd have her bent over the sofa with her skirts over her head, and damn but she deserved more respect than that.

What the hell is wrong with me?

Wrenching away, he held her at arm's length. "Perhaps we shall continue this later tonight."

She nodded as she wiped the moisture from her lips. "I look forward to it."

As he fled the room, he cursed himself for a nodcock. What sort of man had a new wife full of curves and fragrant skin at home that he wasn't bedding with regularity? Yet how could he do exactly that when he wasn't sure he could trust her again?

Why was everything suddenly so convoluted?

Stapleton Boxing Salon
Mayfair, London

HOW LONG HAD it been since he'd stepped foot into the salon? At least two weeks, for it had been before the bout that had caused all his problems.

The second Duncan came into the Stapleton Salon, the familiar scents of sweat, fresh straw that filled some of the punching bags, and the oils they used for the leather mittens brought him back to all the times he'd spent there or with his father, learning how to better himself within the sport.

His brother Alexander came out of the back office and lifted a hand. "Fancy seeing you in here today. Lessons to the public don't start for another hour."

"I know." Or at least he thought he knew. Everything was still a bit murky. "I, uh, needed to come in, reacclimate myself to the cornerstone of my life." Then he blew out a breath. "As well as work out some pent-up tension."

"Ah. I know what that means, but since this gives me an excuse to leave off with the damned ledger books, I'm happy to give you advice if needed."

"I'd appreciate it."

"Newlywed life not going well? I mean, damn, when Lydia and I married, I swear we spent most of that first week in bed, and…" Alexander's words trailed off when Duncan narrowed his eyes. "And that must mean you and your bride are still working things out."

"Shut up, Alex. It's complicated."

"Relationships usually are." When Duncan didn't answer, his brother continued. "Have you regained all your memories?"

"Most of them, I think. Of course, I wouldn't know which ones are missing." Though he chuckled, the sound didn't contain much mirth, and there was more bitterness there than anything else. "I'm glad you and Lewis weren't there to see my defeat." Yet if they had been, he would have never met Phoebe or have been tossed into the murk that he currently struggled with.

"From what I heard, you were holding your own up until the end."

Duncan shrugged. "He was simply a stronger opponent. It's a wonder I wasn't killed."

"You'll come back better next time." Alexander frowned. "I assume you'll continue to do the bouts?"

"I will, especially now." He had greater responsibilities, and they pressed in on him. As his memories continued to return and strengthen, he grew ashamed of them. And oddly enough, he didn't know if he wanted to be that man any longer, for that man would disappoint Phoebe. Even though she'd lied and basically held him captive in a life he didn't lead, he missed the simplicity of that existence… when he had her.

"What do you want to start with today, then? Sparring or the bags?"

"Anything would be useful at this point." As he spoke, Duncan removed his top hat and greatcoat. He dumped them onto a wooden chair resting near one of the walls. "I can almost hear the questions sitting on the tip of your tongue. Out with them." The sooner they had the conversation out of the way, the faster he could move on.

Alexander rubbed a hand along the side of his face. They were very much alike, he and his brother, that they could pass as twins, and had often played tricks on professors at Eton when they were younger. "I can't believe you're a married man."

"You and me both." He struggled out of his jacket of green superfine. It landed atop his outer garments. "But it could have been worse, I suppose."

"There is that." His brother looked at him with speculation. "And physical relations between you are...?"

"Strained. Non-existent, really." As heat went up the back of Duncan's neck, he wrenched off his waistcoat of tan corduroy. "I'm still annoyed with her for meddling in my life and for trapping me into a marriage I never wanted."

"Yet you spent a week with her in Surrey, for all intents and purposes a content man with a wife, working at a bakery." Alexander's lips curved with a cheeky grin. "I can't believe it, but to be fair, once Lewis and I realized you were missing, we were quite frantic."

"You should have come looking for me sooner." Had no one cared?

"How the hell were we to know? Half the time you either keep to The Albany or you're with one of your lady friends, and since you were in a snit with us for doing more of the responsibilities here, we assumed you were making a statement by not coming by." He dropped a hand on Duncan's shoulder. "I'm sorry. We should have been more perceptive." The same sentiment reflected in his brown eyes.

"It's all right." He nodded and then stripped off his shirt. Once he'd tossed it away, he moved toward the line of leather punching bags. Two were filled with sand for the more experienced boxers and two were filled with packed straw. "What am I to do with my wife? The more time I spend with her, the less likely I'll be to bed her."

"Then do it." Alexander snorted. "You're married. There's no scandal in it."

"How can I when I'm not sure if I trust her?"

His brother laughed as if that were the largest joke. "So then all the other women you've taken into your bed have had that for you?"

"I won't dignify that with a response."

Alexander hooted again. "The fact that you're struggling over this means you must have cared deeply for her, and that's why you are taking the betrayal so hard." He shrugged. "Remove the lies and start at the feelings. Those were real. Besides, I truly don't believe she was after a title or a boost into society. The poor thing seems quite genuine and mortified about what happened." He sobered, and there was compassion in his eyes. "Now she'll be thrust into society with absolutely no training. Mama is helping, but it's a tall order."

And why the devil had their mother taken a special liking to Phoebe, anyway? She hadn't shown nearly that same affection to his brothers' wives. He stiffened his spine. "It's Phoebe's own fault."

"Perhaps, but she *did* take care of you when you went missing. Tended to your wounds. Looked after you. Dare I say loved you?" One of his eyebrows rose in question.

Heat went up the back of Duncan's neck. "She lied to me."

"As if you haven't done that in your life."

"She told me we were expecting a baby." He maneuvered behind one of the bags filled with sand while his brother stood close and held it so it wouldn't swing. "The odd thing? I was ecstatic at the news." Then he threw a punch into the bag. Damn but it felt good to return to this sort of exercise he truly enjoyed. "I thought I would have a family of my own." Did it sound pathetic to admit that? Not knowing, he pummeled the hell out of the bag with quick strikes and jabs.

"I don't doubt you did, which is why you have taken issue with everything. Can you imagine yourself with a child?"

He shrugged, not trusting his voice, for the loss of that tiny hope—even if it had been a lie—put a ball of emotion in his throat.

"I firmly believe you loved her." Alexander frowned. "She taught you about her world, helped you to acclimate to it, built a life with you when you didn't know who you were. When you were naught but a stranger to her. It was a huge a sacrifice and a commitment for her. In many ways, I'm in awe of that."

"So am I, damn it." Punch, punch. "What she did was wrong."

"Perhaps, but she did what none of us could do."

"And what was that?"

Alexander flashed a cheeky grin. "Bring you to heel. And what was more, you went willing. Hell, I think you'd let her lead you on a merry chase if you were so damned stubborn."

What was there to say about that. "Do shut up."

For the next quarter of an hour, he gave himself up to punching the bag with varying degrees of force and different styles of punches, jabs, and upper cuts. The dull sound of his fists connecting with the taut leather was quite satisfying. And it helped him think.

Eventually, his brother broke the silence. "Do you still harbor those feelings for her?"

"How can I? Everything was a lie. Everything we had together was a lie."

"Was it? Or was the lie only when you bedded her and truly felt something for a woman for the first time in your life? That you have spent countless hours denying to yourself? Because you are afraid that if you truly fall, she might not return those feelings, and you don't wish to look the fool?"

All valid points, and they only helped to order his thoughts slightly. "I don't know. *How* could I know?"

"God, you're nearly gone over her, I'd say, even if those feelings came about in an unconventional way." Alexander shrugged. "Why don't you simply ask her?"

He frowned and gave the bag one more punch. His knuckles were red and hurting, for he hadn't wrapped his hands, but it was a satisfying ache. "Why do you care?"

"I want you to be happy, to have what I do with Lydia, what Lewis has with Cecilia. Marriage isn't a prison sentence when you're with the right person. It's more freeing, or rather it enhances what you already were and makes a man… better."

Was that true? Is that what he felt when in Phoebe's company? "Bah. I was already quite exceptional."

His brother snorted. "Yes, an exceptional arse. Right proper one too." Alexander nodded and winked. "Do you still wish to be that man?"

That question so closely mirrored his earlier thoughts that he gawked a bit at his brother. "I don't know."

"Now who is dissembling?" Alexander gave him a knowing look. "Will you ignore your wife and take a mistress?"

"I can't say at this time." The time he'd shared with her in Surrey went through his mind then jumped to how he wanted her even now but doesn't know if he can trust her. Did it matter all that much? Could they merely build upon what they already had together?

"Are you upset that she lied or that you enjoyed the life you had with her?"

"It's complicated." He gave the bag another few punches.

"Ah." Alexander moved away from the bag so that Duncan could work with it while it swung for the added challenge. "Consider the situation from her viewpoint. Phoebe truly didn't know who you were, so she couldn't exactly have written to anyone, nor could she turn you out on your own, where you would have been put into danger." He paused as he met Duncan's gaze. "That has to count for something. She has a good heart, and she's truly suffering because of it." He blew out a breath. "Give her latitude, brother. Letting yourself fall for her is a lesser crime than some escapades you've embroiled yourself in. Domestication could be just the thing you've needed."

This was also true, and mimicked some of his own thoughts. "I suppose I *should* find out if she knows how to dance."

"Indeed." Alexander's expression brightened, and it made

Duncan feel a bit lighter as well. "Lydia and I are throwing an autumnal rout in a few days since she's really taken to being a viscountess. Bring your wife. Mama's helping her with a wardrobe. It can get Phoebe's feet wet in society. She'll be among friends, which will assist in tamping down nerves."

"Thank you. I will." He nodded. "The longer I punch this bag, the more my memories of boxing come back. That brings me comfort, for it is a vital part of myself I was missing."

"Excellent news!" His brother grinned. "Will you tell your wife that you have another bout this weekend? I assume you aren't dropping out."

Truly, he'd forgotten that with everything else. "I'm still in good shape, and God knows I could use the prize purse if I win. The enormity of needing to take care of a house and a wife isn't lost on me."

"Good. Lewis will be pleased, and I promise, we will both be there."

A sense of peace fell over him. "Hell, perhaps I should announce it at your rout. Isn't that what you fellows did with your wives to make them fly into a pelter then ultimately accompany you? Why skew tradition?"

"Now who's being cheeky?"

With a grin, he gave the bag another punch. "Partner me. Let's see if I still have skill against an opponent."

"Ha! This might be my only chance to knock you out," Alexander joked as he stepped away and began to remove pieces of clothing.

"Or make me blissfully unaware again," Duncan said in a low voice. That was the only way his heart would cease to ache.

Wasn't it?

Chapter Thirteen

October 24, 1817
Stapleton Boxing Salon
Mayfair, London

PHOEBE FROWNED AS she stood on Brook Street, staring up at the façade of a building that housed a shoe seller's shop. There was a tiny sign on the second level that proclaimed the existence of the Stapleton Boxing Salon, but as of yet, she hadn't ventured forward to find stairs that would lead to the salon. To be frank, it was somewhat disconcerting to be here by herself in the rapidly darkening evening, but her husband assured her that it would be safe and that at least one of his brothers would be in attendance.

In order to discover that, she would need to find the courage to go upstairs. Why was London so big and frenetic and loud? It sapped at her confidence.

"Lady Frampton?"

She turned at the sound of her voice, and her heart gave a glad leap to see Duncan's middle brother striding up the pavement toward her. "Oh, Viscount Wexley, how lovely that you're here." Immediately, a wave of relief went through her person.

"I suppose it is," he said with a grin, "but why are *you* here? It's not every day a lady lingers on the street outside the salon."

"Well, since I wanted to know more about Duncan's world and why he loves boxing so much, he asked me to meet him here once the salon closed for the evening." With a frown, she glanced about, but other than the viscount, there was no one else in the vicinity. "I must admit, I still haven't acclimated to London's hustle and bustle. It's quite overwhelming and I often find myself drowning in the differences from Cranleigh."

"I can only imagine what you're going through, and a pox on Duncan for not taking you around to see the sights so you'll grow accustomed to the noise and crowds."

"He, ah, is good at avoiding me." Even she heard the disheartened note in her voice. "Except this morning. For whatever reason, he woke in a different mood."

"Oh? How so?" The viscount led her to the side of the building and through an ordinary door, which opened into a narrow wooden set of stairs.

"Well, for one, he kissed me as I was enjoying breakfast, then he told me about the rout you and Lydia are hosting, and lastly, he invited me here." She shrugged. "That is a large step forward for him, since this is a big part of his life that he's previously shut me out."

"Agreed." He opened a door at the top of the stairs then let her proceed him into what appeared to be an office. "It is progress, so let us be grateful for that." When he came into the room, he closed the door behind him. "This is Lewis' office, but it's also where I keep the books for the salon. At times, the countess will assist in that endeavor, especially if I'm busy on the salon floor or with private lessons."

She glanced around the space that had been tastefully decorated in a masculine style with heavy oak furniture and gleaming floorboards. A window at the opposite side of the room looked out into the salon itself, due in part of the open Venetian blinds. Overall, there was a sense of power housed in the room, and she could easily imagine the brothers inside, planning their monthly schedule.

Then the door leading into the salon opened. The earl came into the office, and when he saw her, he gave her a ready grin.

"What an unexpected surprise. Welcome, Phoebe."

Faint heat went through her cheeks, for she enjoyed how the brothers used her given name while in private but her title when in public. "Good evening, Your Lordship."

He snorted. "Lewis, please." When she nodded, he continued. "What are you doing here? Duncan didn't tell me to expect you. And, in fact, I'm on my way to the Lords."

"I was told to meet him here since I'm curious about this part of his life, but for whatever reason, he's late."

"Then, by all means, let Alexander and I show you around the salon." He went back into the salon proper. "Out here on the floor, we have much going on at any given time. The general public is allowed inside later in the afternoon, but we'll also do paid lessons across the room on the tick mattresses." With a hand, the earl gestured to a corner where a small ring was roped off. "Then there are the punching bags on the far wall where clients can practice their punches and jabs or gauge their strength."

Alexander caught them up near the bags. "We also offer sparring lessons."

She frowned. "What is that?" Everything was new to her, and it made her thoughts spin.

"When both opponents wear stuffed, leather mittens and punch each other. The mittens prevent serious injury or bruising and allow clients to get comfortable with the act of boxing." He grinned. "I can teach you if you'd like."

"Oh, I don't know…" Not in her wildest dreams did she ever think she could punch someone, even during a lesson.

"I think you'll like it," Alexander said with plenty of teasing in his voice.

The earl nodded. "It might help you to understand why Duncan enjoys it so much, especially since he's fighting in another bout this weekend."

"What?" It felt as if the bottom of her stomach dropped to the floor. "He didn't tell me that." A wave of hot annoyance rose in her chest. "After the horrific outcome from the last one, why does he think he'll have a different outcome now?"

Both brothers exchanged a speaking glance.

"That is a largely unfair opinion." Annoyance flashed in the earl's eyes. "Duncan has raw talent and is quite skilled when he's in the ring."

"Lewis is correct." Alexander was no less aggravated, and she appreciated their need to defend her husband. "Couple that with the fact that he's desperate to make coin to support you."

"What?" Again, she was left breathless by something they said.

"It's true," he continued. "Duncan wishes to do right by you. We spoke at length yesterday regarding his new marriage and what he wants for the future."

Would he tell her that, or would that betray a confidence? A queer little tremor went through her heart and encouraged flutters into her lower belly. Then her spirits plummeted. "While that is admirable, of course, the sad fact is that Duncan doesn't care for me, though."

"Not to be rude, but come off it, Phoebe," the earl demanded, and when his intense gaze landed on her, she took an involuntary step backward. "My brother cares for you more than you think, and for him to tell either of us anything about his inner thoughts, it means you have been uppermost on his mind."

Her heartbeat accelerated. "But he hasn't said anything to me, and we haven't done…" Heat burned through her cheeks. "Well, nevermind. That's a bit too personal, and I need to remember talking with you is *not* the same as doing such with my aunt."

Both men chuckled, and the awkward tension was soon dissolved.

Alexander briefly touched her arm. "Then Duncan is a fool."

"Thank you." However, her inadvertent admission buoyed

her confidence.

"Come with me." The viscount led her over to the wall near where large, long leather bags hung suspended by ropes from the ceiling. "Since Lewis has got duties to parliament, and since Duncan is late, I'll give you a first lesson into boxing. Then you can truly stand up in defiance to our little brother."

A snort of laughter escaped her. "I have already done that a couple of times, to no affect."

"That you know of," Lewis was quick to remind her as he trailed behind them.

Alexander was quick to choose a pair of brown leather mittens, then one by one, he held them up for Phoebe to shove her hands into. "These will prevent errant punches from landing hard into my face," he said with a fair amount of teasing in his voice.

"As if I could ever do that."

"It happens," the earl said as he rested a shoulder against the wall with his arms crossed at his chest. "Alex always thinks he's immune since he has a pretty face."

The viscount made a crude gesture at his brother, and they both chuckled. Then he rested his attention on her. "You'll form fists as best you can while you land your punches into my palms."

"And remember, your middle knuckle will guide the direction of where your fist goes," Lewis added as Alexander guided her a bit away from the punching bags. "It will feel odd at first, but you'll soon acclimate to it."

For the next several minutes, Phoebe learned how to form a fist as much as the somewhat stiff mittens would allow and how to throw a punch. Where she assumed she wouldn't have the strength to drill her mittens into the viscount's hands, she surprised herself when not only did she do it, but the power and confidence such exercise filled her with was amazing.

Eventually, her husband entered the boxing salon from the public door, and as soon as he saw what she was doing with his brothers, he immediately joined them. Annoyance and jealousy warred for dominance in his expression.

"What the hell is going on here?"

"What do you think?" the earl was quick to answer with a faint grin. "Your wife came by to meet you, and since you were nowhere to be found, Alexander decided to teach her a few basics of boxing."

Only then did she realize Duncan carried a small bouquet of autumnal flowers wrapped in dark yellow tissue paper. "You brought flowers?"

"Yes." He nodded and with a shrug, he held them out so she could see the asters, chrysanthemums, daisies, and other blooms all of orange, yellow, white, and red colors. "I thought you might enjoy them, and wherever you put them in the house will add some much-needed cheer."

Her heart squeezed. "They are quite pretty, and it's a lovely gesture on your part."

As he glanced at his brothers, Duncan rested the bouquet on a nearby wooden chair. "I will take care of the remainder of the lessons for today, if you don't mind."

"Of course." Alexander winked at her. "I have accounts to fuss with in any event."

"And I am headed to the Lords for the night," the earl said as he crossed the room toward the office.

"Let's graduate you to the punching bags," Duncan said as he moved her toward those items. As he went, he snagged a pair of leather mittens and began tugging them on, using his teeth to tighten the laces. "We'll start you with one filled with straw."

"Do you think I'm ready?"

"It seems like it." As he offered a grin, she gave him one in return. "I witnessed some of your punches as I came in, and they were quite impressive."

"Thank you."

He stood behind one of the leather bags and held it steady. "Just like you did with my brother, guide your punches but hit the bag. You can alternate your fists as much or as little as you'd like."

"All right." Slowly at first, Phoebe punched the bag. Her mitten-covered fists landed differently into the bag than they had in the viscount's palms, but it was no less satisfying. "Where have you been?"

He frowned but was no less appealing, for a shock of his light brown hair fell over his forehead. "To be honest, I had to hail a hack since I haven't got 'round to renting a conveyance yet, but I had the driver meander through Mayfair, which gave me time to think. Then I bought you the flowers."

"Did your thoughts clear?"

"A bit." Silence reigned between them as she continued to punch the bag. "Why are you here?"

"You told me to meet you here this evening."

The sound of his chuckle sent tingles down her spine. "No, I mean why are you in mittens and indulging in boxing lessons?"

"Oh." Heat filled her cheeks. "I wanted to understand the world you come from, and since boxing is in your blood, I thought I might find out why."

Surprise jumped into his eyes. "You did that, for me?"

"Um, rather because of you. Since you immersed yourself into my world—not of your choosing—I wanted to put myself into yours, hopefully as a way to draw closer to you." Was admitting that a weakness?

"I'm humbled you feel like that."

The way he looked at her sent heat scudding through her blood. Because of that, Phoebe missed a punch to the bag. She lost her balance, tripped between two of the bags, and went on to land a mitten into his chest. "I didn't mean to do that." Yet nearly being in his arms again was heady stuff indeed.

He was so close, so very close, she watched his eyes darken to the color of molten chocolate as he steadied her. "Defend yourself, Lady Frampton." With each word, his lips brushed hers. "Let's indulge in a bit of sparring." Then he gave her a gentle tag on the shoulder with his right mitten.

"Oh, dear." Her heartbeat accelerated, but she followed his

lead and gave him an experimental tap to his chest with one of her mittens.

"Nicely done." Duncan threw a punch that landed on one of her mittens. "Do it again."

For the next several moments, they exchanged blows and punches.

"I know you have banked emotions. Use them to exert more force in your punches. Make me retreat. Go on the offensive," he encouraged with a tiny nod.

"I will try." As she thought over the events of the past two weeks, it was easy to summon the necessary energy to funnel into her fists. One powerful punch tagged him on the shoulder, and he looked at her with admiration and heat in his eyes. "Ooh. That felt… lovely."

He nodded. "Keep going. It is one reason that I adore boxing. Usually, it keeps me sane."

"I'm beginning to understand that." Over and over, Phoebe threw punches, and when he taught her a more effective way to jab, she incorporated that movement into her routine. At one point, she tried an uppercut, which was one of the things Alexander had showed her, and she clipped Duncan's chin with the tip of her mitten.

"Nicely done, Lady Frampton." A bit of awe wove through his voice, but he gave no quarter and made her defend herself.

Sweat formed on her brow and upper lip while she continued to lash out at him with her mitten-covered fists. With each punch, she gained strength, and soon she was moving her feet in time to the movements of her hands. So much so that he was forced to retreat even as he blocked her blows and gave some of his own.

"That's it. Keep yourself steady and don't use all your stamina at the beginning of the fight. Bank it for the final round, for that's when you'll need it most."

The sound of leather slapping against leather filled the immediate space around them.

And still Duncan retreated until a wall at his back prevented further movement. They came to a halt near what appeared to be a broom closet.

Elation rose in her chest. "Does this mean I've won?"

"I rather think you have." With a grin, he unlaced the laces with his teeth then pulled off the mittens. "Do you have any other questions about boxing?"

"I do." So much happiness flowed through Phoebe's veins that she had a difficult time not hopping about like a rabbit. "Why do you do it? Your brothers told me you are scheduled to fight in a bout this weekend. It's so soon after your last injury that I can't imagine why you would take on an additional risk."

"Ah." Shadows filled his eyes as he shrugged. Then he tossed his mittens to the floor. "I suppose there is a certain rush or madness to it. I gain strength from the roar of the crowd who come to watch." While he spoke, he prowled toward her. "Boxing is an art form, but it is also exercise and a way to earn funds. Beyond that, practicing the skills and doing bouts is a way to continue my father's legacy."

She nodded. "Will you tell me about him some day?"

"I will." The heat had returned to his eyes and fired her own.

"I think, as well, you like to win when you're in a match."

The grin he flashed had the power to weaken her knees. "Perhaps. I made a rather poor showing the last time, so this one I have to prove that I'm not a failure."

"You're not. At least I don't think so."

"Mmm." It didn't matter that he didn't appear convinced, for he hooked a hand about her nape, pulled her against the strong, hard wall of his chest, and then treated her to a string of intense kisses.

And she melted further into him while clinging to his shoulders, the mittens she still wore behind his head. There was something different about him this evening, as if he'd come to a decision with himself and had stopped wrestling with his thoughts. There was a certain hunger, an insistence in this embrace that hadn't been there since that seemingly long-ago night when they'd coupled in Surrey. So glad was she that he was more like the man she'd known before that she nearly sobbed with relief, but instead, she kissed him back as if her life would depend upon it.

"Damn, but I want you," he whispered against the shell of her ear before dragging his lips along the side of her neck. "Would that we were alone." The cheeky man cupped one of her breasts, teased the nipple into a stiff peak with the pad of his thumb through all the layers of her clothing, and chuckled when she softly moaned.

The clearing of a masculine throat had them both springing apart, even though they were married.

Though her brain was far too passion-fogged to allow an instant return of thoughts or even a verbal response, she glanced at Alexander as he stood off to one side.

"You know, Duncan, as a rule we don't allow scandal in the salon." The viscount winked at her.

Remarkably, her husband laughed, and the rich sound of it warmed her chest. "Oh, as if both you and Lewis haven't been intimate with your wives here. And before you wed them, I might add."

A flush went up Alexander's neck. "I can't argue with you."

Despite herself, Phoebe laughed. "Oh, you men are so fortunate in that you have each other. I'm glad for you."

Duncan looked askance at the viscount. "Don't you have somewhere else to be?"

"Yes, home. In fact, I want to close the salon so I can spend time with Lydia. I'll drive you both home if you'd like."

"Very well. We'll be right there." Duncan nodded as he unlaced Phoebe's gloves and then tugged them off her hands. He met her gaze while his brother walked away. "You seem at peace, relaxed. Are you?"

Phoebe nodded. "I am, which is surprising. The exercise is rather lovely, but it's more than that." She briefly bit her lower lip. "I adore having a family again. I've missed that so much."

"Sometimes, my brothers are far too aggravating for their own good, but I wouldn't give them up, even when I'm cross with them." He slipped a hand about her waist and led her over the salon floor toward the office where Alexander waited. "Do you know what our cook has planned for dinner? I'm quite hungry."

"I don't, but does it matter? You'll probably eat whatever she puts in front of you." Her husband had quite the healthy appetite.

"No doubt I will." Again, he put his lips against her ear. "And I have a feeling food is not the only thing I'm hungry for tonight."

"Oh." Heat went into her cheeks, but she couldn't help her smile. "I look forward to seeing where the rest of the night will go, then."

Was it possible they'd moved past the hurdle of lies that had kept them apart? Dear heavens, she hoped so.

Chapter Fourteen

Later that night

DUNCAN HAD SENT Phoebe upstairs nearly an hour ago with the bouquet he'd brought her in the boxing salon. Of course he would join her, but he wanted a brandy to calm his nerves and to remove something from the small safe in his study.

He glanced at the flat, rectangle-shaped box lying on his desk. The maroon linen cover had long ago faded, but it was one of the physical things his father had left him in his will, and it was one of a handful of items that wasn't tied to the estate so couldn't be sold once his father had debts mounting up.

With reverent movements, Duncan opened the box. It was a parure of jewelry, all delicate silver filagree work set with oval-shaped sapphires and aquamarines, and on the necklace, smaller diamonds. The only piece missing was the ring that currently rested on Phoebe's finger that he put there at the nuptial ceremony.

And now he was going to bestow the remainder of it to her. It was time to start treating her like his wife in every way that mattered. What was more, he rather suspected that he'd finally untangled his feelings for her. They hadn't changed overly much since their time in Surrey. In short, he *did* love her. He hadn't realized it until earlier tonight while sparring with her. After running his fingertips over a few of the stones, he softly closed the box, swallowed the remainder of his brandy, then stood.

Would she appreciate the offering? More than that, would she know what it meant?

A few moments later, he arrived at their shared suite. As quietly as he could, Duncan opened the door and closed it behind him. In the event she had already retired, he didn't wish to disturb her. "Phoebe? Are you here?"

"In the bedroom." The dulcet tone of her voice worked to further calm him. "Where were you? I assumed you would have come up sooner."

"There was something I wished to attend to in the study." As he walked through the sitting room, he left the box of jewelry on the top of a bureau. Then he removed his cuffs, collar, and cravat. At the connecting door to the bedroom, he toed off his boots and let them fall to the hardwood with dual thuds. "There is something I want to gift you with, but I'll do that a bit later."

"That's not needed. You have already given me so much." She smiled at him from the midst of a mound of pillows in the middle of the wide four-poster bed. One of the windows was half-open, for she craved fresh air, and he couldn't deny her that even if it wasn't a popular choice in society. The steady drum of rain sounded in the room and brought with it the scents of autumn—wet leaves, smoke from chimneys, and the smell of the world that was preparing for slumber ahead of winter. It was quite inde-scribable but familiar.

He shrugged. "What can I say? You are my wife, and I want you to have lovely things."

"Ah." Phoebe laid aside the book she'd been reading. No doubt she'd procured it yesterday during her outing with his mother. Her smile brightened the room and caused his heart to squeeze. "If you're not careful, your brothers will tease you and say you're in danger of tossing your hat over the windmill for your wife."

"Is that such a bad thing?" At the last second, he decided against declaring himself. Perhaps that could wait for later as well.

"Not necessarily." Slowly, she slipped from the bed and stood. With her hair loose and flowing about her shoulders, she was every bit a siren. Clad in a night dress with a matching wrap, both in a shade of light blue trimmed with lace that hugged her curves, it was clear she didn't have sleep immediately on her mind. "I enjoyed being at the boxing salon with you tonight." Her pink toes peeked out from beneath the hem of her dress as she came toward him.

"So did I. Perhaps we can have a few private lessons soon." He snaked an arm about her waist when she drifted close. The faint scent of lavender and vanilla teased his nose. "Would you like that?"

"I would." Her grin widened, and his world temporarily tilted. "You have the look of a man who has made a decision and is better for it."

He frowned. "Perhaps I have." Did he have the courage to speak to his feelings a second time? Would she hurt him again? His focus fractured when she laid a palm against his chest. The ring he'd given to her at their nuptial ceremony winked in the soft candlelight. In a few moments, he would have her in his bed, and if he were fortunate, they wouldn't leave until well after the sun rose tomorrow morning.

"Duncan?" One of her blonde eyebrows rose, but amusement sparkled in those stormy blue-gray eyes he adored. "May I ask something of you?"

"Of course. Anything." He trailed a hand down her back, and the heat of her seeped through the thin night clothes.

"Could you see your way to…" A nervous giggle escaped her. "That is to say, do you think you might try to…" She tugged at the buttons on his jacket of green superfine. "Put a babe in my belly? A real one, so we might be a real family?"

"What?" He could scarcely breathe from the sudden overwhelming emotions that crowded into his throat. "Me, a father. It has long been a dream." Duncan stared, unable to immediately comprehend the magnitude of how their lives might change. Did he trust her enough for that? "I… are we ready for that next step?"

She laid a palm against his cheek. There was nothing but honesty and hope reflected in the blue pools of her eyes. "We were going to couple tonight, were we not?"

"Yes, but—"

"And you weren't planning to withdraw or even wear a sheath, correct?"

"No, of course not, yet—"

"Then falling pregnant might be a natural side effect of enjoying each other's bodies, yes?" A trace of tears rose into her eyes. "Please, Duncan. We are married. I truly believe you and I have a chance of enjoying a lovely union, but I need to know that you trust me… after everything."

"Well, damn." Why couldn't he adequately speak his emotions? Not knowing the answers as he struggled, Duncan laid his hand over hers, turned his head, and then pressed a kiss into her palm. "Yes, I trust you." Since meeting her, he'd experienced a world much different than his own, and he craved that simplicity. "I am learning how to be a better man… because of you." The muscles in his throat worked as he tugged her into his arms and held her.

"Does that mean while we are figuring out how to work together as husband and wife, you might wish to be a father too?" she whispered into his ear.

Did he? When he thought back to that week in Surrey when he'd thought he would have that very dream and how wonderful it had made him feel, how he wanted to feel that again, he slowly nodded. "Yes. I would like that, and… I want that life. To make you proud of me."

To make his family proud of him.

"Oh, Duncan." Holding his head between her hands, Phoebe pulled back enough to peer into his eyes. "I am that already, and the more time we spend together, the more I know what an amazing man you are, and will be."

"Thank you. That means so much." Damn, he never realized

how much he needed someone in his life to believe in him, just as he was.

She rose onto her toes and pressed her lips to his. "Never let anyone make you feel small or tell you that you don't matter because you aren't doing something *they* think you should. *That* is the lie."

A trace of moisture went into his eyes. "I appreciate that… appreciate *you*." Then, because he couldn't stand it another moment longer, Duncan settled her back into his arms and kissed her, drank from her, showed her without words how much she meant to him. Tangling his hands into her long, blonde tresses, he urged her head backward and deepened the embrace.

Silk slid along satin as their tongues danced and dueled. Tiny fires erupted through his blood and that heat fueled his hunger for her. Easily, he tugged at the ties of her robe and urged it from her shoulders. The thin material fell with a whisper to the floor. Her fingers plucked at the buttons of his jacket. A low growl escaped him, for he was obliged to break the kiss to shed the garment only to toss it to the floor. Phoebe slipped behind him with a throaty giggle, where she worked the ties of his waistcoat and helped him off with the piece of clothing. He didn't offer a protest when she yanked the shirttails from his breeches. Then her fingers glanced over his skin beneath the shirt, dancing, stroking, caressing, and he thought he might die from the heaven of that touch.

It was what he'd craved since they'd come together in Surrey.

"Phoebe…" Both needing to feel her everywhere on his person and not wanting her to extend the torture, he removed the shirt. "I want you."

"I haven't bid you nay, Frampton." The way those sultry tones uttered his title had his shaft hardening faster than if she'd teased it. While she held his gaze, Phoebe slowly, so damn slowly, took off the thin night dress. When it pooled on the floor at her bare feet, a breath shuddered from him. "Do you think you'll delay any longer?"

Oh, dear God.

"I rather doubt it." His shirt came off in record time, but the breeches proved problematic when he got a foot stuck in one of the legs. She watched him with a mix of amusement and desire in her expression, but finally he had the foot free and kicked out of the garment. Seconds later, he joined her beneath the bedclothes and covered her body with his.

And it was like being welcomed home all over again.

The warmth of her called to him; the faint floral scent of her teased his nose. "I adore how you feel." Her whisper in the room with the rain in the background enhanced the intimacy of the moment, but it was her fingers on his back, tracing a few scars he'd garnered from boxing that completely broke down the last of the doubts he'd harbored. "In the event you wondered, you are enough." She peppered the underside of his jaw with kisses, nipped a line along the column of his throat.

Emotion shivered through him, and for a few seconds, Duncan buried his face in the crook of her shoulder. Growth was difficult and painful at times, but he welcomed the opportunities to become a better man—for her, for them—to start building a family together.

This time while he made love to her mouth, he teased a breast with his hand. A moan sounded from the back of her throat and her back arched, for she particularly enjoyed it when he worried her nipples.

"Tonight, I refuse to be denied." Phoebe urged a hand between their bodies. When she cupped his shaft and stones, he sucked in a breath, for he was so hard that he might pop off at any moment. "I can't help but marvel about this part of you."

Oh, God.

Her touch was both heaven and hell, but he didn't bid her nay. Pleasure pulsed through his veins, concentrating in his length. With every stroke, with each brush of her fingers, he was hurled closer to the edge of bliss. Needing a distraction, Duncan delved a hand between her splayed thighs. Easily he encouraged the swollen nubbin at her center out of hiding, and seconds later after strumming his finger over it, circling it, alternating degrees of friction, his wife uttered a strangled sort of scream as she fell into a gentle release.

"So responsive." It was but one of the things he adored about her. "And we have only just begun our journey together."

"Must be the naughty company I keep." She squeezed his stones and chuckled at his moan. Just as he thought to play at her nubbin again, her fingers glanced over the highly sensitive skin that rested between his stones and anus. The giggle she made when he nearly launched off the bed echoed in his ears.

"Where the hell did you learn that?" He'd assumed only courtesans knew that secret about a man's body.

"Oddly, your mother gave me a few tips the other day."

"God, I do not want to think about that, or anything surrounding that conversation."

She snorted with laughter. "Then why don't you finish me? I don't wish for extended foreplay tonight."

"As if I could deny you anything." As it was, he was nearly out of his mind with need. He rested the bulk of his weight on his forearms while aligning his tip at her opening. "You're sure?"

"I am." She looped her arms about his shoulders, wriggled into a better position, and bumped her hips against his. "And I haven't had nearly enough of you."

Bloody hell but he was so damned fortunate he could hardly bear it. Had his brothers felt the same way after they married their wives?

There was no more time to set aside for thinking. Desire and need took command. With a powerful flex of his hips, he penetrated her body, went as deep as he could. Their moans of enjoyment blended with the rain. She was still so damned snug that they were truly fused as one.

The bite of her fingernails digging into his biceps competed with the bite of her teeth when she nipped at his earlobe. He gripped her hip with a hand and encouraged one of her legs upward with the other, which allowed him to stroke ever deeper into her honeyed heat.

Over and over again, Duncan thrust, and she matched his rhythm until they moved effortlessly together in a dance as old as time. The second he peered into the blue pools of her eyes, saw the same emotions reflected there that were flitting through him, he was lost, and he knew that he would never stray into another woman's bed, for he had finally found contentment with her.

But did she truly love him? She hadn't said the words… yet neither had he.

Eventually, he passed the point of no return. Urgency roared through his shaft and tingled through his stones. Every tiny little sound of encouragement pushed him closer to shattering, and when she slipped a hand down his back to squeeze one of his arse cheeks, he was gone. "Phoebe!" The hoarse shout sounded overly loud, but he didn't care. The servants would need to understand that this was the first of many couplings he intended to have with his wife.

"Oh, yes. Go harder. Faster."

How could he deny the request? With the last of his strength, he stroked into her with short, deep, fast thrusts until he thought he might completely expire from either the effort or the pleasure beginning to flood his person.

Finally, her body stiffened. A keening cry left her throat. Phoebe arched her back, gripped his arms so tightly he feared she'd leave bruises. Her thighs quivered. Like a litany, she repeated his name, alternated it with the word yes. The words became his mantra, pushed through his blood, and then with one powerful stroke, he went tip over tail into the void of bliss where nothing existed except extreme, soul-shattering sensation that made him feel comforted, satisfied, and as if he'd somehow perished at the same time.

"Well, damn," he whispered against the side of her neck as he came back to himself. Sweat dampened his back while he struggled to regulate his breathing.

She chuckled, but the sound held an edge of exhaustion. "I enjoyed that and will require another round soon." As she drew a hand along his chest, the tickle of her fingers through the sparse hair there nearly sent him to heaven once more, if that was even possible.

"I am glad you're so satisfied. With everything." When his wife nodded, he flashed her a tired grin. "Give me an hour and I'll show you the depth of what I'm feeling."

She bussed his cheek and then burrowed into him while wrapping an arm about his waist. "Oh? Why not tell me now?"

"I... uh..." Where were the words when he needed them? Perhaps he was reticent for fear it wasn't love at all that he felt. After all, the past two weeks had been quite a whirlwind. "How about I let my gift talk instead?"

Why am I such a coward?

Before she could answer, Duncan slipped from the bed. He crossed into the adjoining dressing room, retrieved the box of jewelry, then returned to the bedchamber. This time, he alighted on the side of the bed and handed her the box.

"This is one of the only things my father left to me in his will. I don't know if he wished for me to give it to my wife or if he wanted me to sell it, but I held onto it all the same." His voice broke only a bit. "Now, I'm giving it to you. It's the parure your ring came from."

"Oh?" She struggled into a sitting position, and then with a shaking hand, Phoebe opened the lid. A gasp escaped her. "Merciful heavens, this is beautiful, but far too much."

"Not for you. In fact, I wish I could give you more—everything. But that might need to wait until I can make something of myself."

"These will match my gown for tomorrow night." She touched the stones of the necklace with her fingertips. Then, with a frown, she met his gaze. "We have a house, servants, and each other. For a girl from Cranleigh, this is already quite a boon." When she leaned forward and put a palm against his cheek, a shuddering sigh escaped him. "And, because of you, I now have a family. I don't need anything else."

If he wasn't careful, he'd tumble right into those shimmering eyes. "Except a baby?"

Remarkably, a blush stained her cheeks. "There is that."

"And we might have a child before either of my brothers. I don't believe either sister-in-law is with child yet." The idea of finally beating Lewis and Alexander at something tickled him and made him feel even closer to her. "Just know you are becoming far too dear to me, and that nothing in that box is as valuable as I believe you are." It was the best he could do in this moment, but eventually he'd say the words.

When the time was right.

"Oh, Duncan." Tears welled in her eyes then fell to her cheeks. "Are you certain I'm worthy of any of this?"

His heart squeezed hard. "Of course." He took the box and laid it on the bedside table. Then he joined her in the bed and pulled her against his body beneath the counterpane. "Sweeting, if you think I'm worthy as I am, then how can you doubt that you are as well?" He pressed his lips to her temple. "In an odd way, we will be—are—good for each other, and we will both succeed *because* we have each other."

"*This* is the man I remember, and you make me so happy I'm a bit fearful it might all dissolve again," she said in a choked whisper, as she put her arms around him and pulled him down for a kiss.

There was no doubt this time that he was willfully and completely lost in her. There would be time enough to gather his courage on the morrow and tell her what was being etched on his heart. In the meantime, he set out to kiss her senseless and worship her again with his body, for at least in that way, he knew he didn't need bravery.

Chapter Fifteen

October 25, 1817
No 10
Bedford Square, Mayfair

P HOEBE HAD BARELY entered the drawing room before the butler appeared at the open doorway. She greeted him with a smile. "What it is, Peterson?" A week with her staff—how had she become a lady with servants?—and it was still awkward for her to think that people had been employed to wait on her.

What would my mother say if she could see me now?

The butler, a man of indiscriminate years, nodded. "The Dowager Countess of Lethbridge is here to see you."

"Now?" Knots of worry pulled in her belly. "Lord Frampton and I are to leave for the rout soon." In fact, Duncan was in the process of finishing his toilette with his valet.

He shrugged. "I couldn't say, my lady. Shall I send her up?"

"Yes, please." Phoebe nodded. She smoothed her gloved hands down the front of her navy silk gown. Hundreds of tiny clear glass beads had been sewn onto the skirts so that she twinkled each time she moved. A sprinkling of small silver spangles had been sewn along the scooped bodice, and her silver satin slippers matched that embellishment.

Whyever was her mother-in-law here?

In a few moments, the dowager swept into the room clad in a

gown of russet-colored silk. "Good evening, Phoebe. The navy hue suits you."

She couldn't help but smile, for she felt like a princess. "Thank you. You are lovely tonight as well, Regina."

The older woman nodded. "The gown was a wonderful choice with the necklace." Then she turned to the butler. "You'll need two footmen to take two trunks out of my carriage. I've brought some bric-a-brac items for your curio cabinets, a few pairs of draperies if you'd like to change colors at the windows, and a gown for you of bronze taffeta because it will set off your blonde hair and blue eyes, Phoebe." She waved a hand at Peterson. "There are also a handful of paintings in the carriage. I thought Lady Frampton could have them hung in this room. They were of particular interest to her husband's father."

"Of course, Your Ladyship." Then the butler departed.

Then the older woman rested her attention on Phoebe. "I hope you don't mind, dear. Starting out housekeeping when one is young is sometimes difficult with no coin."

She nodded. "Duncan is doing his best."

"He always does, but I fear the boy will become distracted. I want your home to be elegantly appointed for the time when the pair of you host your first event."

Oh, dear heavens. I hope that isn't any time soon.

"Thank you for the assistance, but why did you decide to bring such things over tonight? We're to leave soon for Alexander's rout."

"I wanted to see how you faired before you and Duncan went out, but now we can ride together." She tugged on the edge of one glove as she glanced at Phoebe. "Dear, why do you seem so green about the gills?"

Something about the older woman's composure made her envious. "I'm so nervous about tonight. Dancing isn't my strong suit. I've barely had any lessons. My parents didn't put much stock in such things as they assumed I'd never have cause to use those skills." She heaved out a sigh. "And I've never been in society, not even in passing. I fear I'm going to embarrass Duncan and quite possibly the whole Stapleton family."

After you have all been so kind to me.

"Well, no doubt that *will* happen."

Phoebe gasped. "What?"

"It happens to every one of us, even me a few times." The dowager softened the comment with a mischievous grin that made the lines framing her mouth and eyes a bit more prominent.

"Truly?"

"Oh, my, yes." Amusement twinkled in her brown eyes. "Though I was the daughter of an earl, I was reared within society and the rules therein. I thrived in that life and in that social circle, but when I was a young bride, everything changed."

Drawn into the story, Phoebe drifted a few steps closer to her mother-in-law. "How so?"

"For one, George was quite handsome." The older woman tittered. "In fact, Duncan resembles him quite heavily. So I was distracted in those days." She nodded. "Four months after I wed him, we appeared in public as a couple for the first time. My husband had just come into the title—in fact, when we returned from our wedding trip, his father unexpectedly died from an ailment of the lungs—and he was anxious to show the *beau monde* that he'd married well and would be successful as a new earl."

"What happened? I can't imagine you as anything as elegant." It was the truth, and one of the reasons the dowager intimidated her.

"It was a summer ball hosted by a duke, and I remember it being quite steamy that evening." Her eyes took on a faraway look as she reached back into her memories. "Combine that with my being both excited and nervous, with my husband determined to prove himself worthy of the title so was being gregarious than usual, and the fact that I was naïve and didn't know I was increasing at the time, and it was one big brewing storm."

"Oh, dear." Phoebe put a hand to her cheek. "What happened?"

"I vomited all over my partner during the steps of a Viennese waltz. Unfortunately, it was the very duke to whose home we were invited." The dowager chuckled over the remembrance. "I was mortified at the time. So much so that I refused to leave my townhouse for a full two weeks afterward. My husband was beside himself with worry and frustration, but it wasn't until the duchess paid me a call and told me that her husband found it amusing that I relaxed enough to show my face again."

"I don't know if I could overcome something like that," Phoebe admitted with a tiny shake of her head, but some of her anxiety eased. "Retching is so unpleasant to begin with."

"It certainly is," Duncan said as he came into the room, looking extremely handsome in his requisite dark evening clothing. There was something special about seeing a man in satin knee breeches and a tailcoat that set the heart to fluttering. "Of course, when I speak from experience, it is usually because I've imbibed in too much brandy."

The dowager chuckled. "While that is true, I'm impressed by the way you've reined yourself in since your nuptial ceremony. It is almost as if you are a new man."

"Perhaps I am." He went over to his mother and bussed her cheek, then he did the same to Phoebe. "I didn't know that being a husband would practically demand that I change."

She frowned at him. "I appreciate it, though."

"I haven't said I minded," he added, with a wink. "We should go else we'll be late, and I don't wish to do that to Alexander."

"You're right." The dowager moved toward the door as she resettled her gold wrap about her shoulders. "I'll tell the butler to have the carriage brought around."

Once she left the room, Phoebe glanced up at him. "Again, I want you to know that I didn't want you to change so terribly much that—"

"Shh." He cupped her cheek with a gloved hand and tipped her head backward. "I hadn't, truly, but I think we can both agree that limiting vices is something we can both be glad about." Before she could answer, he brushed his lips over hers then pulled away with a soft growl. "That kiss won't be enough to assuage my desire, but we are obligated to attend this rout."

"Oh!" She couldn't help her giggle. "Then let us make certain we don't linger tonight, hmm?"

There were times when she adored having a husband... despite the challenges.

No 6 St. George Street
Hanover Square, Mayfair
Westminster, England

WITH A PLEASANT sort of ache in her muscles and her breathing a bit shallow, Phoebe laughed as Duncan escorted her over to the side of the drawing room. As soon as dancing commenced twenty minutes ago, he'd partnered her in a country reel, and miracle of miracles, she knew all the steps to the dance.

"That was more fun than I had anticipated," she confided to him with a hand on his arm. "I only stumbled twice."

"You were remarkable out there." He slipped a hand about her waist, and then at her ear, he whispered, "And you are quite the looker in that gown. More's the pity we aren't alone."

Heat went through her cheeks. "I appreciate the compliment, for the gown is lovely; your mother has been generous with her time and coin."

He waved a hand. "For whatever reason, she has taken a liking to you. Which is odd. I don't recall her ever doing the same with my brothers' wives."

"Then perhaps she feels sorry for me. After all, I'm not of the *ton*, and she's probably wondering if I have any manners at all. Perhaps she's waiting for me to make a mistake." The knots of worry were back in her belly.

"Nonsense." As a Viennese waltz was announced and couples filled available spots on the makeshift dance floor, Duncan took one of her hands. "I think Mama genuinely likes you. We should all be grateful for that. She didn't take kindly to Cecilia at first, and when Alexander announced his intentions to court Lydia, she wasn't pleased."

"That's disheartening in and of itself, for those ladies are infinitely better suited for this life than I am." She shook her head as a feeling of inadequacy came over her. "Unless she didn't hold out much hope for you and has accepted the fact that this is as good as you can do."

Am I not good enough, then?

"I'm sure that isn't true at all." He drifted the fingers of one hand over her cheek regardless of whether they were in public. "But if you are truly worried, I can broach the subject with her."

"Oh, please don't do that." A heavy sigh escaped her. "We shall see how things go." Then the waltz was underway, and she sighed again, for a different reason this time, for she might have enjoyed partnering with her husband during that set.

"Are you disappointed we aren't joining in?" he asked in a low voice.

"A bit, for you are so handsome tonight, I would have like to know what it felt like to be partnered with such a striking figure." Why was she such a ninny? "I might also have your undivided attention during the set." After that last coupling between them, something had changed within her. Truth to tell, she was quite certain that she'd fallen in love with him, but he hadn't said the words to her again to her since that time in Surrey.

As himself, and she desperately wanted to hear them.

"What makes you think you don't already have my undivided attention?" The intensity in his brown eyes and the way the natural wave in his hair caused it to run riot over his head without care to a popular style all worked at sending tingles to the base of her spine.

"Oh?" Why did she persist in doubting him? Was it because of how their relationship had begun, with her lies? Had he only bedded her because he had urges and they were married anyway as a way to retaliate?

He led her out of the drawing room and then scooted her away from the open doorway and out of the view of the guests. There was no one else in the corridor with them. "Shall I show you how it's taxing my control not to throw you over my shoulder and spirit you upstairs to an empty room right now?"

Another round of heat went through her cheeks. "Uh, I—"

Her husband didn't allow her the time to finish the sentence, for he trapped her between the wall and the hard obstacle of his chest, cupped her cheek, and then lowered his mouth to hers. It wasn't a usual gentle kiss, oh no. This embrace had far too much steam behind it, and as he moved over her lips, explored every millimeter of them, teased them with his tongue, Phoebe slowly lost her grip on reality. When he probed the seam, she gladly opened for him, and all too soon, their tongues were dueling, battling, and silk slid against satin as the embrace progressed.

As the strength of her knees turned to that of cooked porridge, she curled her fingers into the lapels of his tailcoat merely to stay upright. It should be a crime for a man to be that handsome and have such skill in kissing.

When he finally let her up for air, he remained pressed against her with his arms wrapped around her and keeping her upright, grinning down into her eyes. "Did that remove any doubts from your mind?"

"It made strong inroads into building my confidence," she responded with a whisper with a thought that she might melt into a puddle at his feet.

"You seem a bit heated." He gave her a cheeky wink as he eased away. "Perhaps I should fetch you a glass of champagne, hmm?"

Oh, goodness, that was a treat she'd never had before. "I would enjoy that. There isn't much need for such a drink in Cranleigh."

"All the more reason for you to experience that luxury now." He took her hand, brought it to his lips, and kissed the back. "I shall return shortly. Perhaps you should return to the drawing room before someone comes searching for you."

She could only nod like a silly goose, for her mind refused to form words, and when Phoebe went back into the drawing room just as the waltz came to an end, she could have sworn that her feet didn't even touch the floor. When Cecilia waved to her, she waved back, and seconds later, the countess joined her.

"You seem as if you are enjoying yourself tonight, Phoebe," the other woman said, with a ready smile. She was quite resplendent in a gown of marigold satin.

"I am, and what's more, I didn't expect to since this is the first time I've been in society." With a glance around, she located Lydia, who was talking to her husband and hanging onto him in a somewhat scandalous manner that warmed her heart. When her gaze caught that of the dowager's, she smiled, and was pleased when her mother-in-law did the same. "It is quite a different world in the *beau monde*."

"I understand that all too well, but you have only been married for a week. Give things time, and I'll wager you'll find that you have more in common with everyone here than not." Then she winked. "And I suspect your husband won't let you fall into embarrassment. It helps that he's entirely too handsome for his own good."

Phoebe nodded. "One thing is certain. The Stapleton brothers are certainly easy on the eyes." Did she just say that aloud? A giggle followed, for it wasn't as ridiculous as it sounded.

"I agree." Cecilia came closer and dropped her voice to a whisper. "They are quite possessive and intense when it comes to carnal endeavors."

"This is so true," she said with a nod and as a wave of heat swept over her.

"What is true?" Duncan asked as he joined them and put a flute of champagne into her hand. "Good evening, Cecilia."

The countess smiled with a confidence Phoebe envied. "We were merely discussing the fact that this rout is proving to be a success." Then she waved. "Lewis is trying to catch my attention, so I will talk with you later."

Once she left them alone near the wall, Duncan softly clinked his flute to hers. "Why do I have a feeling neither one of you are being truthful?"

She grinned. "Would you rather have heard that we were discussing the virility of the Stapleton brothers?"

A dark flush came up his neck over his cravat and collar points. "Where did I rank?"

"Do hush, Duncan," she said with a mock smack to his chest. Then she took a sip of the champagne and giggled. "Oh, that tickles my nose, but it is lovely."

He winked. "Welcome to the *ton*, Phoebe. I have a feeling you'll make your mark soon." Then he took a deep sip of his own sparkling wine.

"That remains to be seen." She tasted the wine again, and decided she enjoyed it. "I have worries regarding your bout. When, tonight, will it be?"

"In a couple of hours. I think around midnight. Even the promoters won't flaunt society's rules and hold it on Sunday morning, proper." He watched her as he sipped his champagne. "Don't worry. I can hold my own."

Except the last time, he suffered temporary amnesia. "Who is your opponent?"

"I don't know. Since I have been distracted from that world by you, I have no idea who is on the roster." Briefly, he put his lips to her ear. "And lest you think that is a bad thing, it is not."

Heat was in her cheeks again. "Are you certain you are strong enough, in the right mindset for another bout so soon after your last injury?"

"Yes." He drained the remainder of his drink. "I'm well enough and feel good. Don't you have faith in me?" The cheeky man dared to kiss her temple.

"Oh, you." The bubbly wine tickled her nose and made her head feel far too fuzzy. "Do you truly believe you can win the match?"

He sobered. "I'll do my darndest. We need that coin."

"Why?" She couldn't help her frown.

When he shrugged, it highlighted the breadth of his shoulders. "As you hinted at last night, you want a babe in your belly, and I'm rather inclined to think that is a jolly good idea."

"Oh?" Phoebe stared at him as shock filtered through her. "You wish to be a father?"

"I'm ready, I think. I wanted that life in Surrey, was crushed when it was all a lie, so now that we're rubbing along well again, why shouldn't we move our lives forward? I want to experience everything that I can while I'm able, for my father died far too young."

"I know that sentiment well." Tears welled in her eyes. "I would like that very much."

"Good." Then he looked at her with so much desire in his eyes, that she wondered if anyone else could see it.

"And as for the bout…"

"Yes?" His expression was guarded as if he expected her to demand he not go.

She laid a hand on his chest. "I'm not letting you go alone. I will be there cheering you on tonight, for no longer are we at odds." At the last second, she bit off what she truly wanted to say. Later, she could tell him of her feelings. "You'd better remain in one piece with your full faculties, because I'm not nearly done with you."

A hoot of laughter escaped him, and his eyes sparkled with amusement. "Why, Lady Frampton, does that mean you have plans for me after the bout?"

"What do you think?" She winked, and felt far too uninhibited. "After all, I *do* enjoy seeing you half-clothed…"

"Ah, Phoebe, I want you so much, but that will need to wait until at least tomorrow."

"I know, but you are worth waiting for." The feeling of falling returned.

His mother drifted over with a smile. Alexander accompanied her. "The two of you seem quite cozy together. Are you enjoying the rout?"

"Very much so." She took another sip of champagne then frowned. "However, it is unfortunate that Duncan must leave early."

"What?" The dowager appeared shocked. "Why? Is he ill?" She focused on him. "Are you well?"

He shrugged. "Everything is fine. I have a bout later tonight; you shouldn't be surprised, for both Lewis and Alexander left society events early for the same reason early in their relationships. And you know even boxing organizers don't run them on Sundays."

Phoebe frowned. "Did you not tell your mother?"

"Oh, dear, he tells me absolutely nothing," the dowager said then she sighed. "I suppose I can't blame him, for I have been fairly critical of all my boys."

Duncan snorted. "Yes, slightly," he responded with heavy sarcasm in his voice.

Alexander laughed. "Well, this time, Lewis and I are going with you."

"As am I," Phoebe asserted with a nod. "At least I'll be able to watch him in action."

A long-suffering sigh came from the dowager. "Perhaps we should all go, since last time ended in disaster."

"Indeed." Alexander winked. "Shall I tell Lewis we should leave and to have the traveling coach ordered?"

"Yes, please, and I'll go with you," the dowager said.

Then Duncan blew out a breath. "Was it such a disaster the last time? After all, it did lead me to marrying you."

"Perhaps, but I will still worry over you until the bout is over."

"All will be well. I promise." And he took her flute from her fingers then laid both pieces of stemware onto the silver tray of a passing footman. "There is much living to do afterward."

Still, she would send up a prayer for him while they were en route.

Chapter Sixteen

Later that night
Near Ashford, Surrey
England

"GOOD GOD, LOOK at the crowd," Duncan whispered to his brothers as he swept a glance about the wildflower field where the bout would be held. Lewis would serve as his corner man—which meant he wasn't allowed in the ring—but he would act as support and give advice or discuss strategy during the bout. Alexander would try to get the crowd to throw their support behind Duncan as well as serve as his knee man, which essentially meant he'd offer his knee between rounds for a rest. Dear Phoebe had volunteered to take care of the water bucket and ladle, offering it up when needed. "It's bigger than when I fought two weeks ago."

Lewis snorted. His gaze was on the gathering crowd as well. "Once word got out that you would fight again after your sound defeat two weeks ago, they wanted to gawk and perhaps wager against you." He shrugged. "Pay them no mind. This is your chance to have a comeback as well as a victory. Let them wonder and put a hole in their coffers."

"Thank you." Illumination from lanterns hung from the ropes that designated the boxing ring gave off cheerful pools of golden light. "I'm glad the two of you are here, though. Already, it has a much different feel from last time." Countless other lanterns had been strung up in the many trees throughout the area, as well as tall poles erected and secured about the roped-off area so the men in the crowd would be able to watch the fight in the dark. It gave the area a surreal quality, as if he were on a stage instead of a ring.

Lewis clapped a hand to his shoulder. "We've all learned lessons over the past two weeks, I think. Stapletons stick together, no matter what. Papa would have wanted it that way."

"We never know what life will show us to be thankful for," Duncan murmured, as he wandered to the corner that had been set aside for him. Behind the wooden post that had been driven into the ground, Phoebe stood, clad in a long black cloak. It wouldn't hide the fact she was a woman, in a ballgown, no less, but it would protect her identity and reputation. "Thank you, also, for wishing to watch the fight."

"Where else would I be?" Her eyes glittered in the lantern light. "The last time you did this in Surrey, you wandered about Cranleigh with no memories. I can't risk some other woman snapping you up if it happens again." Though she smiled and had said that in jest, the note of worry in her voice went straight to his heart.

"That is not going to come to pass. You have my word." Slowly, he removed his tailcoat and then his waistcoat as both brothers joined him in the corner. He handed the garments to Alexander. "No matter what occurs in this ring, do not come under the ropes, else I'll be disqualified, and it will become yet another scandal. Understand?" he asked of his wife.

"Of course." She nodded, but her overbright gaze remained glued to him as he shed his cuff, collar, and cravat. Those items went into Alexander's keeping as well. "Be careful."

"I will." Finally, Duncan took off his lawn shirt. Once he'd given it to his brother, he began the task of taking off his shoes and then the hosiery. "Did you remember to bring the satchel of clothing I had in the coach?" It was something he'd brought with him when they'd departed for the rout.

"Yes." She retrieved it from the grass and gave it over to him. "Why did you need it?"

"Well, I'm damn well not going to enter a bout in satin breeches. They are far too expensive to destroy with such exercise, and will restrict movement." So saying, he took off the garment and handed it to her. He didn't care much about standing in the nude; there was no place for modesty at a bare-knuckle boxing match.

Yet Phoebe's gaze travelled down the length of his naked body, and his member twitched with interest. She stepped against the ropes and lowered her voice while his brothers turned politely away. "I'll never tire of that view, but I suppose you'll return to me tonight battered and bloodied, hmm?"

"No doubt I will." After yanking a pair of tan-colored breeches from the satchel, Duncan quickly donned them. "But I *will* come home to you."

"I know." She nodded her thanks when Alexander gave her the pile of Duncan's clothing. "Your mother is waiting in the coach. She couldn't bear to witness her youngest son in the ring."

"Her constitution isn't as strong as yours, but I'm glad she's in the immediate area for support." His chest tightened. "Mama always says I resemble Papa the most. I'd rather not provide more trauma for her, since Papa died after a fight." The crowd cheered because his opponent had entered the ring, along with the men serving as judges and a doctor. Once more, his gaze went to Phoebe, who had put his folded clothing on top of the satchel, and tucked everything nice and tidy into the corner behind where she stood. "I *will* make you proud."

Her smile was a tad watery. "I am already proud of you, Frampton. Just stay alive."

"I'll do my best."

"It's almost time," Lewis said in a low voice as he clapped a hand on Duncan's shoulder. "Remember what Papa taught us. Footwork will win the day."

Alexander swore under his breath. "But fast fists will ensure it," he said with a grin. "Bring the man down any way you can. That I learned from Lydia's guidance."

"I now wished I'd learned jujitsu like you did." Duncan flashed a grin at the people he loved most in the world. "Thank you all for coming with me tonight. It means the world."

Then a shrill whistle blast pierced the air. It was time.

"Good luck," Phoebe whispered with a fleeting touch of her gloved fingers on his arm.

Heated tingles danced up to his elbow. Damn, it was rather lovely having a wife, someone who truly cared about him. "I'll need it." Yet his confidence in his own skill surged to the forefront. Everything his father had taught him rested front and center in his mind.

With a little shove from Lewis, and an encouraging nod from Alexander, Duncan slowly made his way to the center of the boxing ring. The crowd roared again. He narrowed his eyes on the mountain of a man who was his opponent—Mr. John Burlington. Built like a barge and standing perhaps a few inches over six feet, he featured a barrel chest, broad shoulders, and a narrow waist. Dark brown hair was long and caught back with a leather tied. A thick mat of matching hair covered his wide chest. Anticipation glittered in his hooded eyes beneath shaggy eyebrows, and there was no doubt in Duncan's mind this man wished to evict him from this mortal coil.

"Just give up now, Lord Frampton," his opponent growled as he slammed a fist into the palm of his other hand. "I ain't afraid of your lineage."

"You should be. Stapletons are difficult to kill."

"Gentlemen, keep it civil. We don't want a bloodbath before we even start." A squat, rotund man stood in the middle of the boxing square and held up a hand. He had the look of a fat bird in evening clothing. "I'm your caller tonight."

Both Duncan and Burlington nodded.

"Limber up. We'll begin as soon as our host introduces you."

When the noise from the crowd died down somewhat, another man stepped into the middle of the boxing ring. The tall man, of indeterminate years and build, held up a hand for silence.

"Tonight's match is between one of the favorites of the bare-knuckle boxing world, Mr. Duncan Stapleton, or you may know him as Lord Frampton, and one of the best boxing promoters I swear I've ever had the pleasure of meeting."

A roar erupted from the men assembled as spectators.

"And his rival, the man who's beaten countless boxers throughout the southern counties of England, Mr. John Burlington." Another cheer rose from the crowd. Clearly the man had supporters.

With a frown, Duncan stretched his arms and neck. It didn't matter which one of them had more supporters. He would do what he was capable of and make his wife proud, show her that he was more than capable of earning a living and taking care of her. When he risked a glance back at his corner, his gaze met Phoebe's. She stared back with rounded eyes and her lips set in a hard line in a pale face surrounded by the dark hood of her cloak that blended with the night, but she gave him a nod of encouragement. Both of his brothers stood with their arms crossed at their chests with stoic expressions, but they were there, and he swore he felt that love.

When he turned his attention back to the two men in the ring, another man had entered the ring to stand next to the caller and the announcer. Oddly, they resembled the number 10, with one being tall and the other squat. The third back, landing somewhere in the middle of the two, held up a hand for silence.

"I am Mr. Jansen, your judge for the bout this morning." The man had the look of a London banker, somber in a dark suit with dark hair and hardly a personality. "The bout will continue until one of these fighters pins his opponent for ten seconds, or one of them manages to knock the other out cold."

A roar from the crowd followed. Spectators of bare-knuckle fighting were a bloodthirsty bunch, and the more battering or gore presented, the greater the wagering.

Another man stood at the far side of the ring, outside the ropes, with a black bag in hand. No doubt he was the doctor in the event things took on a horrible turn.

Duncan's opponent again smacked a fist into his other hand. "I heard about your last bout, Frampton. I'll put you down just like your last rival." The accent of a southern fisherman clung to the man's voice.

Hot annoyance surged through his chest. "That was a one-off experience, Burlington. You'll have so such luck." He flexed his hands, cracked the knuckles then performed a series of stretches to warm his muscles. It was already quite nippy in the air, and he needed his body loose and limber.

The bigger man snorted. "The wins in my column are greater than yours. There's talk the Stapleton brothers aren't as good as they brag these days."

"We'll see. A boxer is only as good as the fight he's currently in." Sad but true. Again, he glanced over to his corner where Phoebe was quietly talking with Alexander. His heart squeezed to know she was there, and she believed in him. When she looked over his brother's shoulder at him and smiled, confidence surged through his veins.

"The bout will start in moment," the judge said.

Another roar from the crowd followed.

When the three men left the boxing ring, Duncan assumed his first position, fists at the ready, body taut and balanced, just like his father had taught him. "Good luck, Burlington." After all, no matter who was declared the victor at the end of the bout, he would still be proud of himself merely because he had Phoebe. The prize purse would be welcome, of course, but loving her? That was the real prize he'd found on the heels of that bout two weeks ago.

A whistle blast split the air. The judge shouted, "Remember, rounds will continue until one man is put on the ground and unable to stand after ten seconds. Go!"

The crowd roared in anticipation.

Chapter Seventeen

D UCAN AND HIS opponent circled each other, prowled through the dark meadow grass of the eight-foot roped off area. The multitude of lanterns cast eerie shadows over the ground and gave the bout an otherworldly feel. The doctor as well as the caller walked the outside edges of the ring. What was the best way to bring down a mountain? Then he grinned to himself.

One bloody rock at a time.

Even though patience wasn't his strong suit, he pulled all that he had around himself. With his father's voice in his head, he threw the first punch. It connected solidly with Burlington's cheek, but the bigger man didn't seem to notice. Clearly, he considered Duncan like an annoying mosquito.

The other man grinned as he struck out a powerful fist that clipped Alexander's shoulder, almost spun him around. "Come, little man. I expected more from a Stapleton."

"So do many people, but we can't be all things to everyone." Damn, wasn't that a truth he should have learned earlier in life? He danced away, much to the crowd's roar of approval then Duncan swung a fist, but the bigger man easily dodged the punch.

"This bout will be mine." Burlington struck with a fast uppercut to his chin that jarred Duncan's teeth together. He followed it with a jab to Duncan's middle. "I'll be known as the man who put the youngest Stapleton into an early grave."

"Shit." Pain exploded through his face and stomach, but he held his ground and returned the volley, tagging the bigger man in the chin and abdomen. And because he was a bastard, he slammed a knee into Burlington's groin. When the other man bent over with a cry of pain, Duncan once more delivered a punch to his opponent's chin.

Which Burlington didn't like. Then they were into the thick of the first round as blows rained and fists pummeled, landing on solid flesh in rhythmic intervals. Shadows danced and the lantern light had the capability of blinding him, but Duncan refused to give ground. The thud of fists hitting skin echoed in his ears. The roar of the crowd built up his confidence. One of his right hooks had Burlington staggering backward, but the giant didn't fall. He seemed rather frightening in the golden illumination.

But then, neither did Duncan hit the ground when Burlington few back at him.

Minutes ticked by that seemed like hours. Blood trickled along the side of his face from a wound that had opened at his right eyebrow from one of his opponent's blows. His breath grew labored, but he defended himself. A quick jab to his lower lip had the metallic taste of blood flooding his mouth, but he kept his feet before the round was finally called.

Grateful for the brief reprieve, Duncan trudged to his corner, as did Burlington. Winded, he sat on Alexander's offered knee then spat blood from his mouth. "Burlington has stamina, I'll give him that." He met Phoebe's gaze in the lantern light. "Are you doing well watching us beat each other like we've got no sense?" It hurt to chuckle.

"I'll admit, it's both thrilling but disgusting."

From outside the ring, Lewis snorted. "The man's a force, this is true, but if you'll watch closely, he favors his left knee. And his weight doesn't make him as light on his feet as you."

"Listen to your brother," Phoebe said softly as she handed him a ladle full of cool water from an oaken bucket. "He's been examining Mr. Burlington non-stop since the bout began. He and Alexander believe you can take him down in the fourth round sheerly by tiring him out."

"I'd rather knock him out, but he's massive." But he nodded. "Thank you."

"Focus." Alexander gave his shoulder a shake. "You are letting his size intimidate you. Papa was larger than you, but you managed to take him down during sparring once. Keep your strikes fast and low then use your power for punches to the head. Use your strength to run him around."

"Makes sense." Duncan wiped sweat from his brow with a rag. "Thank you." After taking a deep sip of the cool water from the ladle, he handed it back to Phoebe. "I appreciate your support."

"Where else would I be?" she said with a shaking smile.

"Enough of that. You can romance each other later." Lewis kneaded the muscles in Duncan's shoulders. "It's bare-knuckle boxing. If you can't bring the beast down in his torso, use the bad knee to your advantage. Kick the back of it and sent him off balance."

"I trust my skill, but I also know that prize fighting gets a bit dirty."

Another whistle blast announced the start of round two, and with a groan, Duncan stood. He returned to the middle of the ring to face off with his opponent once more.

"I'll pummel you into death, Frampton," Burlington growled. "Not as good a fighter as your father."

"Tell me something I don't know. There is no one like George Stapleton." And perhaps there never would be, but none of that mattered. "I'm going to make his memory proud this night when I take you down."

"You can try, but I'll win the night."

"I don't believe I'll give you that chance."

"Break his nose, Duncan!"

Holy shit. That cry had been from Phoebe, and it warmed him from head to toe. *I'm doing this for her*, he reminded himself. *For us.*

With that small moment of distraction, a hard uppercut to his jaw had him staggering back several steps. The crowd roared. Pain exploded through his face and jawline, but he kept his feet and hoped his teeth weren't broken. With a growl, Duncan lunged at Burlington. He landed a few jabs to the bigger man's stomach, cheek and chin, and then flitted behind the mountain to jam a fist into his ribcage, hoping to bruise a kidney.

The large man reeled and retreated before gathering himself. Seconds later, he charged at Duncan to exchange blows in close combat style.

Again and again, Duncan drilled his fists into the bigger man's body, and in some places on the hard form, his blows felt quite ineffectual; the boxer simply wouldn't fall.

Burlington got off a few good punches of his own, but Duncan had learned his craft well from his father. Quick footwork kept him on his feet and out of the other man's reach. Though he was winded and aching, he was constantly looking for an opening, a weakness. "All that flitting like a butterfly will see you unconscious soon."

"It hasn't failed me before," he said in response. When the pain in various portions of his body became too insistent, he shoved it down and ignored it as best he could.

Annoyance lined the other man's face. "You aren't as good as your brothers."

"That is all in the eye of the beholder, yet I'm still standing. Against you." And he delivered a swift right hook to the other man's cheek that sent the other man spinning about. As the crowd cheered, Burlington stumbled but he didn't fall.

Seconds later, the round was once again called without a clear victor.

I grow weary of fighting a mountain. This needs to end.

Duncan strode back to his corner. He dropped heavily onto Alexander's bent knee, panting. The urge to vomit all over himself was strong, but he willed it away. His body hurt and throbbed with pain; the ache in his head kept up a thrumming pulse. "The man won't go down. It's like literally trying to tunnel into a mountain with a spoon."

"You are going to need to come up with a plan, for he'll wait you out as your strength flags," Alexander hissed, as Phoebe plied him with water. "Dig deeper."

"I'm fucking trying."

"Use his knee against him," Lewis cautioned.

"I tried to get behind him, but he favors it too much."

"Try again, man."

"Right." Duncan stood. He gave Phoebe the ladle. "Perhaps you should go keep Mama company in the coach." The last thing he wanted was for her to see him defeated again.

"No. Don't think to order me away just because you're feeling insecure." When their gazes connected, she offered a tremulous smile but worry clouded her blue eyes. "You are a lovely fighter, Duncan. Don't let him into your mind. If you need motivation, pretend that man wished me harm. If you care at all for me, you wouldn't stand for that." Her voice wavered. "Now go out there and defend against him."

Did she think he didn't care? Damn, but he needed to do a better job of showing that—saying it. "Right." While Alexander wrapped Duncan's battered knuckles with thin strips of cotton, he shared a look with Phoebe. Emotions he couldn't—or wouldn't—identify shadowed her eyes. "I would never let any harm come to you." Heated sensation went through him, followed by a blossom of hope that lifted his flagging spirits. Their future together glimmered just out of sight.

And he wanted it more than anything.

"Get your head out of your arse, Duncan," Alexander demanded as he finished wrapping Duncan's knuckles and palms. "Romance can only happen if you win."

"Indeed," Lewis said with a huff. "Papa taught all of us to fight, and he never believed any of us were terrible at it. We have different styles, and there's nothing wrong with that."

"Put him down like a rabid dog." Alexander gave him a push, which refocused his thoughts.

"Thank you for that." Shoving a hand through his sweat dampened hair, Duncan made his way back to the middle of the ring while the crowd roared its approval, of who he couldn't say.

The judge blew his whistle again. The next round had arrived.

There was no time to think, for Burlington immediately took a swing at him, catching him on the shoulder so hard that he spun about.

"Shit." Pain ebbed down Duncan's arm, but he couldn't think about that right now. All too soon, he was caught up in a whirlwind of blows that left him reeling and very much on the defensive. When one of the bigger man's fists drilled into his gut, pain swamped him, had him doubled over from it. He returned the volley and was fortunate enough that his fist found purchase on Burlington's nose. The sickening crunch of cartilage was satisfying, as was the burst of blood down the bigger man's face.

Scrapping ensued, shoulders locked. Decorum was done for, and that was all the permission he needed.

Releasing his hold on Burlington's waist, Duncan bounced away, using his footwork to runs circles around the bigger man. When his opponent took a swing, he easily ducked, which put the mountain out of balance. Darting behind him, Duncan was quick to jam his heel into the back of Burlington's right knee. The man lurched forward, and Duncan delivered a hard blow to the side of his head. At the same time, he came around and kicked at the wounded knee. That gave him the edge.

With a cry of anguish, Burlington tumbled to the ground, but he wasn't knocked out. The crowd roared from either approval or denial.

"Put him down!" The cry of encouragement from Lewis was

somehow heard over the crowd's noise and the thunder of his pulse in his own head.

"You shouldn't have bragged, Burlington." But before he could deliver another blow, the other man reached out, clamped a hand around his calf and then yanked. Duncan lost his balance with a curse, tumbling to the sweet meadow grass. When the bigger man straddled his hips and grabbed his shoulders in the attempt to pin him to the ground, he fought with all his remaining strength.

"Concede the match, Frampton." Burlington might have strength on his side and the current upper hand, but he hadn't won yet.

"I am not done." Though his endurance wavered, he refused to give up, for he wanted Phoebe proud of him, wanted a future together, wanted to know that contentment he'd had in Surrey with her.

Briefly, he closed his eyes as he fought with the other man to keep his shoulders from the ground. He ignored the yells from the crowd, ignored his brother's calls, ignored Phoebe's pleading. Somehow, he was able to pull up a knee and then gained purchase with his foot to push the larger man from his body. Then he scrambled to his feet, fists at the ready. By the time the mountain of a man lumbered to his own feet, he landed a hard punch to the side of his huge head.

"Fuck!" Burlington shook his head as confusion shadowed his face. He retreated a few steps.

"Who is done for now?" Duncan blew out a breath of pain as sweat rolled down his back. Then he threw another punch, this one landing in the man's breadbasket, and while he tried to recover, Duncan kicked out at the vulnerable knee. Burlington crashed to the ground while the crowd roared. "This bout is mine."

"No…"

With a bit more confidence and ease, he lashed out with a fist, digging his middle knuckle into the man's temple, and followed that up with a left-handed uppercut that connected with Burlington's jaw.

His opponent flew backward to land heavily on his back. Duncan jumped onto him, crawled over Burlington's large form and clamped down on the man's shoulders to keep them from slipping out of his hold. He panted, but when Burlington thrashed about in an effort to break his hold, he hung on.

The crowd roared.

"You are done, Burlington." Knowing the man was truly immobilized, Duncan kept him pinned to the sweet-smelling meadow grass as the larger man's legs flailed.

He stared upward at Duncan with a bit of disorientation in his eyes, but eventually his movements stilled.

"Is that all *you* have, Burlington?" Duncan managed to say around clenched teeth.

"Get… off," the other man gasped out.

"Not a chance."

The crowd roared. His brothers whooped with victory.

When the other man went still in his hold, Duncan continued to keep him pinned. Though blood dripped down his face and onto his chest to mingle with sweat, he looked around at the crowd beyond the circles of light. He couldn't remember how many wounds he'd sustained. Pain screamed through his body, and he sucked in deep breaths.

The judge came over to make certain Burlington was down. When the doctor agreed, the judge counted down from ten.

Then the caller shouted, "The winner of this bout is Mr. Duncan Stapleton! Lord Frampton has taken the prize purse as well as bragging rights for this bout!"

Another roar sounded from the crowd.

Dear God, I've won.

Slowly, Duncan scrambled to his feet. For a few seconds, his world tilted crazily from the exertion, then he bent over and cast up his accounts.

The money is mine.

Nearly a half hour later, he'd finished with all the well-wishers, and as the crowds thinned, he stumbled over to his corner. Damn, but his whole body hurt, and all he wanted to do was seek out his bed and lay in one spot for the next few days.

Or, if Phoebe was amenable, spend those days in much sweeter endeavors.

Lewis was the first to congratulate him. He clasped a hand to Duncan's shoulder. "Fine showing. Papa would have been proud."

"Thank you."

"I'm proud of you too," Lewis said in a soft voice. "You did well out there. The Stapleton name is still a good one."

Alexander nodded. His face was wreathed in a grin. "You're scrappy, I'll give you that, and you made for frantic wagering after the second round. No doubt your cut will be quite fat."

"Not bad for a night's work, hmm?"

"You'll be wanted on the circuit again soon. Are you up for it?"

Duncan shrugged. "Let me think about it for a few days." With a look at Phoebe, he knew all was right in the world when she smiled and offered him a ladle of water.

"Fair enough." Alexander jabbed an elbow into Lewis' side. "You go tell Mama the good news while I claim Duncan's prize purse."

"Thank you." He narrowed his eyes. "That money is going toward my future. My wife and I have plans, you see."

Once both men left the ring, Phoebe dropped the ladle into the bucket. She picked up the pile of his clothing and handed him the shirt. "You were incredible out there. The way you moved, how you kept your feet, knowing that you never gave up..." Tears welled in her eyes. "You are every inch a hero."

"I appreciate that, but I feel like shit for the effort." Donning the garment nearly broke him for all the pain it caused.

"I'll take care of you again; I do have some experience in that." When she offered him the remainder of his clothing, he declined.

"Put it in the bag, but I'll take the boots." When she gave one to him, he shoved a foot into it in some agony. With the second one, a groan left his throat as he tugged it on. "I could only gain that victory because you were here, believing in me."

A tear fell to her cheek. "That has never wavered, never been a lie." Then she uttered a sound that was a cross between a snort and a giggle. "You need to see the doctor."

"Later." As he grinned, pain went through his face. "I'm going to look like a dog's breakfast tomorrow, but I couldn't have done it—everything—without you."

"Oh, I don't know about that." She lifted a hand, danced her fingertips along the side of his face, frowning when he winced. "I am so glad the outcome of this bout was better than the last."

"As am I."

"You could have been killed."

"I wasn't, though."

"Will you fight again?"

"Perhaps. I haven't decided, and I wanted to talk about it with you, because you are my wife."

"Oh." The emotions in her eyes made him catch his breath, and accelerated his pulse. "Is that all you would say to me? After everything we have both gone through over the past two weeks?"

Confusion temporarily took hold of his brain, then he shook his head. "No, it's not. In fact, I have been trying to say those very words for the past couple of days, but apparently, I'm not that eloquent."

One of her eyebrows rose in challenge. "Try. I need to hear the words from the man you are now, today, with all the knowledge you have."

"I understand." When he blew out a breath, his face hurt. "I'm tip over tail for you, Phoebe. Yes, in a mere two weeks, I have fallen in love with you, perhaps loved you in Surrey without even knowing who I was, and I defy anyone to question that. And…"

"Yes?"

"And will you remain married to me? With all the force of love, affection, and respect behind those vows now?" Outside of boxing, this was the greatest moment of his life.

"Oh, Duncan, you are so sweet." Tears welled in her eyes. The drops fell to her cheeks, and she sniffled. In lieu of a handkerchief, she scrubbed at her cheeks with her free hand. "Yes."

"What?" What the devil did that mean? "My brain might have been addled in the fight, so could you perhaps elaborate?"

She chuckled and cried all the harder. "What is there to say, Duncan? I've fallen in love with you as well, and I only just realized it before the bout, but I was certain when you went into the ring tonight, determined to win because of our future."

"A future I desperately want, with you." *Dear God.* He drew in a shuddering breath and let it out. "Does this mean you will be my wife in every sense of the word?"

"I will, and I'll be happy to do so." Phoebe nodded, and her grin could light up the night. "Because I love the man you are. You are perfect for me."

A wave of happiness crashed into him, strong enough to make him temporarily forget about his wounds. "You are exactly the kind of woman I need by my side." He grinned, and his busted bottom lip protested the movement. "Somehow, some way, we will find our way through, and I have a feeling our lives are going to be the talk of Town. Scandal be damned."

"Because it doesn't matter how love comes about, as long as both parties fight for it when they are up against the ropes." She laughed even as she continued to cry. "Now, please, will you go over and let the doctor look at you?"

The dear woman had made a boxing analogy. No wonder he adored her. "How about, instead, we simply go home? There is nowhere else I want to be right now than with you." Then, with a gentle tug, he reeled her into his arms and tenderly kissed her. Even that brought him pain, but he didn't care. "I don't believe I've broken any ribs, and these cuts and bruises won't inhibit any other exercise if you so desire."

"We shall see how you feel after a bath, hmm?" She held him close, and he winced from the pain involved in that. "I'm glad you survived."

"Well, I *am* a Stapleton, and we don't back down in the face of challenges."

"No, you certainly don't. Your whole family has incredible strength."

"Perhaps, but I also believe that strength is from having people believe in us, love us. That goes a long way into making everything bearable." Perhaps that was all a man needed. Love and acceptance led to peace and contentment. "And, sweeting, don't forget that they are your family as well. Always."

"I know." Despite a fresh torrent of tears, Phoebe pulled him close, lifted onto her toes, and kissed him as the hood of her cloak fell backward. Afterward, she held his gaze. "Thank you for giving me everything. How can I even repay that?"

"There is no need, but you can do one thing for me."

"Oh?"

He nodded as he ducked under the ropes with a groan and waited for her to join him. "Give me an heir, not that I have much to bestow upon him, but it's early days yet. I haven't reached my full potential."

But he would, with her help and support.

"I look forward to trying." Then she grabbed his hand and threaded their fingers together despite his still being wrapped with bloody, sweaty cotton. "For now, I only want you."

"I can do that."

With a grin that hurt like the devil, Duncan escorted her toward the area where the vehicles had been parked, where his family waited for him. For the first time in his life, he felt as if he'd finally found where he belonged. No longer did he need scandal to gain him attention or notice. He had that already from one unassuming woman who'd turned his world upside down with lies made from the heart, and what was more, those lies had blossomed into something incredible and pure, something he had no idea he'd wanted all along.

Odd how life worked, and he couldn't wait to see what was next.

Epilogue

May 1, 1820
No 10
Bedford Square, Mayfair

WITH A YAWN, Duncan made his way up the stairs of his townhouse. He'd gone over to Alexander's home for a few moments after his last client at the boxing salon had finished, for he'd wanted to meet his new niece, born barely a month ago. While he'd been there, after praising the baby, he and his brother shared a couple of drinks and talked for a while. Time got away from him, but now that he was home, he was glad for it.

As he always was.

By the time he reached the suite he shared with Phoebe, he had his cravat off. In the adjoining dressing room, he stripped down to his breeches before finally coming into the bedchamber where his wife sat in the wide four-poster bed with their nearly two-year-old son sleeping by her side. Her pregnant belly was hidden by the folds of her satiny nightdress, but that babe would be their third, due by the end of August.

"Am I disturbing you?" he asked in a whisper, as he came fully into the room.

"Of course not." She set the book she'd been reading aside then patted the mattress next to her. "How is your brother?"

He settled where she indicated. "He is still such a proud father. Exhausted, of course, but proud. Lydia is doing as well as can be expected. Since her labor was difficult, she hasn't been up and about much in the last month, but I expect she'll rebound soon enough."

Phoebe nodded. "She's a Stapelton, so she'll rally." She moved into a more comfortable position. "I have four months before this one will make an appearance, but I'll try to call on her in the next few days."

"She'll welcome that. As will Alexander. Especially since Mama is far too busy and distracted with preparing for her second marriage to be a doting grandmother." If there was a touch of bitterness in his voice, he couldn't help it. She'd nagged for years about having grandchildren, and now she was pursuing her own interests.

"Don't be cross, Duncan. Love is love, and your mother deserves happiness again in her life. Once she is wed, she'll pour most of her attention into the children again."

"I know you're right, but it is still a bit annoying." But he couldn't fault his mother. She'd been lonely since his father had died a handful of years ago, and now that her sons were married and not needing her as much, she probably considered herself with free time. Then he peered around her at his son, Edward George, named after both of their fathers. The boy's softly curling brown-blonde hair was as soft as cornsilk. Dark lashes lay against his rounded cheeks as he slept next to his mother. His chin, mannerisms and reckless attitude had all come from Duncan, but his blue eyes were all Phoebe's. "Every day that goes by, I'm continually thankful for what we have in this life." His heart was full, for he adored both of his children equally.

"I am as well." She laid a hand on her belly. "Edward is so curious. I think you'll need to take him to the boxing salon soon to familiarize him early with that part of your life, for it will be his future and your legacy."

That was undoubtedly true, for he had worked in the boxing salon he owned with his brothers for nearly four years. While

Alexander managed it and ran it quite seamlessly, it was Duncan's responsibility to keep investors happy and coin flowing into the salon... while finding backing for the exceptional boxers they launched into the bare-knuckle arena. It was rapidly becoming one of the most popular sports in England, and unless he missed his guess, it would soon cease to be illegal. Frankly, he couldn't wait for that day. And with each sponsorship he sold and with every new investor, he took a cut of that coin, which made for a very lucrative income each year. He and his brothers also conducted private boxing lessons in addition to teaching the general public a few points while in the salon.

"Perhaps, but I rather think it's safer to bring him to Lewis' home since they have the private salon, and his cousins would be happy to see him." He met her gaze and grinned. "I should probably check in on Abigail before exhaustion fully claims me. Shall I take our son up to the nursery as well?"

"Yes, please. He was a bit petulant when the nursery maid put him down, so I had him brought here hoping to calm him, and since I was far too tired to argue with him, I thought this was the best place for him."

Over the years, Phoebe had come into her own within the *beau monde*. In fact, she used the skills she'd learned in Surrey to open two small bakeries around London, and with his investments, they were running flawlessly. So much so that she'd encouraged her Aunt Bess to move to Town to help oversee them. Phoebe popped in when she could around the children's schedules, but with the new babe coming soon, she would need to hire more workers. Especially since her jam tarts had made a bit of a sensation among Mayfair residents.

"You need to rest more. No sense in putting yourself or the babe at risk." Duncan winked. "I'll return shortly." After he gently gathered his son into his arms, he carried him along the corridor to the suite they'd made by putting two guest rooms together. There was one left, and if they continued to have children, they would need to move to a larger home.

There are worse problems to have, I suppose.

Inside the nursery suite, he laid Edward into his crib with a nod to the nursery maid. The nanny, he assumed, had already retired to her tiny room in the attic space. She and the maid often switched off monitoring the children.

"Is all well?" he asked of her.

"It is, my lord," the young woman said with a nod. She looked up from the pamphlet she'd been reading. "Abigail went to sleep without a fight tonight. Perhaps she is moving out of her colicky stage."

"One can only hope." As he quietly moved across the large space to the other crib, he peered down into it and smiled to see the little angel that was his daughter.

As of yet, she didn't have much hair to speak of, and instead had very fine, very pale blonde hairs all over her head. Born in the middle of July last year, she was almost a year old, and though she was plump and petite like her mama, she had quite the temper and didn't like having her schedule upset. In that, she was a bit like her uncle Lewis. Which made Duncan laugh more often than not. She would be a force to contend with when she grew older. Unlike her brother, she had brown eyes, but they were the most soulful pools he had ever seen.

"Enjoy your journey through dreamland, princess," he whispered to his daughter, but didn't dare to touch her cheek for fear she'd wake. Then, with a nod to the nursery maid, he returned to his bedchamber and Phoebe. With a grin, he slipped beneath the bedclothes beside his wife. "They are both asleep and both far too adorable."

"If nothing else, you and I make beautiful children." She leaned over and blew out the candle on her bedside table. "I can't wait to meet the newest."

"Me either." For long moments, Duncan simply held her in the darkness as he listened to the sounds of the house as it settled in for the night ahead. "Once the babe is born, will you consider our family complete?"

"Oh, I don't know." She laid a hand on his naked chest, and just as every time she touched him, his muscles clenched, and desire built. "I might like one more before we should probably take measures to prevent other pregnancies."

He nodded. "Four sounds like a lovely number." Then he slid down the bed, put his hands on either side of her belly, and then kissed the bump through the thin fabric of her night dress. "This is your papa, baby. Your mama and I can't wait to meet you." The fact Phoebe had been delivered of two children already and was growing a third in her belly never failed to astound him.

"Ooh!" Phoebe chuckled softly. "I think the child likes the sound of your voice. It's moving about in there."

"How amazing." When he came up the bed, he once more took her into his arms and encouraged her backward. "Each year that goes by, I fall deeper into love with you."

One of her hands went around his nape. "I feel the same about you, and I knew you would prove a wonderful father. Just as you have been an even better husband."

"I try every day to be a better man than I was before." Who would have thought that nearly three years before, he would have become a married man who had no more interest in chasing skirts or indulging in the vices he used to hold so dear. Of course, the reason he'd done that to begin with was to make his family pay attention to him and to try to relieve ennui. There was no need for any of that, for he was quite fulfilled and content in the life he lived now.

"I'm so proud of you." With gentle pressure from her fingers, his wife encouraged him down for a kiss.

All too soon, he was lost, as he usually was when things turned amorous with her. "I am not the only one doing good things."

"Mmm, but I don't want to talk about me. Or anything, really. I only want to feel you against me, moving inside me."

It was a wonder she hadn't killed him with her enthusiasm, but it was yet another thing that he adored about her, and one of the reasons they were such an exceptional fit together. "As if I could deny you anything," he whispered, as he undid the ties that held her wrapper together.

Life was essentially a mystery where it was lovely then awful then wonderful again, before starting the cycle all over. The key to surviving the upheaval and uncertainty was to just hang on tightly and never doubt the love and support one found along the way.

The End

About the Author

Sandra Sookoo is a *USA Today* bestselling author who firmly believes every person deserves acceptance and a happy ending. Most days you can find her creating scandal and mischief in the Regency-era, serendipity and happenstance in Victorian America or snarky, sweet humor in the contemporary world. Most recently she's moved into infusing her books with mystery and intrigue. Reading is a lot like eating fine chocolates—you can't just have one. Good thing books don't have calories!

When she's not wearing out computer keyboards, Sandra spends time with her real-life Prince Charming in central Indiana where she's been known to goof off and make moments count because the key to life is laughter. A Disney fan since the age of ten, when her soul gets bogged down and her imagination flags, a trip to Walt Disney World is in order. Nothing fuels her dreams more than the land of eternal happy endings, hope and love stories.

Stay in Touch

Sign up for Sandra's bi-monthly newsletter and you'll be given exclusive excerpts, cover reveals before the general public as well as opportunities to enter contests you won't find anywhere else.

Just send an email to sandrasookoo@yahoo.com with SUBSCRIBE in the subject line.

Or follow/friend her on social media:
Facebook: facebook.com/sandra.sookoo
Facebook Author Page: facebook.com/sandrasookooauthor
Pinterest: pinterest.com/sandrasookoo
Instagram: instagram.com/sandrasookoo
BookBub Page: bookbub.com/authors/sandra-sookoo